THE BEAUTIFUL
DEAD END

for Mowry,
who continues to inspire

THE BEAUTIFUL DEAD END

A NOVEL

CLINT HUTZULAK

ANVIL PRESS · VANCOUVER

Copyright © 2001 by Clint Hutzulak

All rights reserved. No part of this book may be reproduced by any means — graphic, electronic, or mechanical — without the prior written permission of the publisher, with the exception of brief passages in reviews. Any request for photocopying or reprographic copying of any part of this book must be directed in writing to the Canadian Copyright Licensing Agency (CANCOPY) One Yonge Street, Suite 1900, Toronto, Ontario, Canada, M5E 1E5

Printed and bound in Canada by Morriss Printing

Cover and book design: Rayola Graphic Design
Cover photos: Vince Klassen

CANADIAN CATALOGUING IN PUBLICATION DATA

Hutzulak, Clint, 1967 –
The beautiful dead end
Fiction.
ISBN 1-895636-39-6

I. Title.
PS8565.U92B4   2001   C813'.6   C2001-910751-X
PR9199.4.H88B4   2001

Represented in Canada by the Literary Press Group

Distributed by General Distribution Services

The publisher gratefully acknowledges the financial assistance of the BC Arts Council, the Canada Council for the Arts, and the Book Publishing Industry Development Program (BPIDP) for their support of our publishing program.

Anvil Press
Suite 204–A 175 East Broadway,
Vancouver, BC V5T 1W2 Canada
www.anvilpress.com

We're everywhere, all the dead of the world. Our final trick, becoming visible again in stone and root and leaf. Translating ourselves into words. Laid out in our dark cloth of letters, spread thin on white sheets, you can see us in any alphabet. Look closely: we are breathing in the spaces between the words.

FRIDAY NIGHT 1

TEQUILA

OUTSIDE, HE REALISES he is not drunk enough. He sits down on the corner of a concrete planter at the edge of the parking lot and rolls a cigarette with his last paper, flips the empty packet of papers beneath a car. He smokes the cigarette down, watching the gas torches along the patio flutter small pennants of flame in the dark. Faintly above the shouts and whistles from the bar he can hear the new highway like a distant river. He carefully pinches the butt out, puts it with the tobacco in the pouch, raises the collar of his blanket-lined jacket against the wind.

Earlier, on the radio in the truck, they were predicting snow over the course of the weekend, and it feels like the weather is changing, some cold front moving down from the north and this is the leading edge. The lighted sign-board trailer has been tied down with cables to big cement blocks on either side so it doesn't blow over. That is new. Someone is thinking ahead, it seems. The cables hum and the dead grass in the drainage ditch tosses and sighs and he can't see it but there is a flag snapping at the top of a pole in the dark somewhere above the bar.

The empty packet of rolling papers comes back at him and he traps it with his foot and looks across the parking lot to the red truck—his truck, as of last night. It's a nice truck: the owner spent some bucks on extras. And the engine. When he'd popped the hood, it was so clean. The guy must have cleaned the damn thing every weekend.

He runs his thumb over the salt-corroded lid of the magnet key box and feels the key slide around inside. He'll have to ditch the truck soon, which is a shame, but the owner will be glad to have it back. He's treated it well; no one could say he hasn't treated it respectfully. With kid gloves, as befits a fine piece of machinery, maybe the first close-to-new vehicle he's ever driven. If he can arrange it, he'll put a tank of gas in when he dumps the truck. As a sign of appreciation. And the key in the magnet box stuck right where the guy will see it. As a reminder to take a bit more care with things of value.

He pulls back his sleeve to check the time and then remembers the watch is gone. Fuck it, he says under his breath, and gets to his feet. He buttons his jacket to his chin and that seems to help a bit, but it's too cold to sit out, and the concrete under his ass has chilled him right through and he has to piss. He takes gloves out of his pockets and puts them down on the edge of the planter and sits on them.

With a blast of music, the woman comes out of the bar. In the shelter of the doorway she lights a cigarette. He sees the flame and then the smoke rising and catching the light from the neon beer sign behind her. She stoops to do something with her boots.

Honey! He stands and calls to her across the parked cars.

She has told him her name only an hour ago and already he has forgotten. She is a friend of his wife — ex-wife, he reminds himself. But he can't remember her name.

She walks toward him, boot heels crunching on grit, her shadow clocking around her beneath the high bronze floodlights.

I thought you'd fucked off for good, she says, stopping in front of him.

I'm like an iceberg out here. He slides an arm around her waist and pulls her to him. Her hair smells of fried food and smoke and hair spray.

Her hand glides over his ass. Poor baby, she says, pouting her lips, tipping her head against his shoulder. You need someone to warm you up? She makes a noise against his chest like a cat purring.

How about we go up to your room, he says, pressing his nose to the top of her head. He likes the feel of her there, close, the leather of her coat still warm from inside.

You call Lillis Rae and tell her you're back to see her? she asks. She taps her cigarette with a fingernail the colour of dried blood. I'm assuming you've called to tell her what's up, right?

I was thinking of it more like a surprise, he says. The cold is cutting through the alcohol and he feels the drunkenness slipping away, his head clearing.

She pulls away and looks up at him, then presses the flat of her hands down the front of her leather coat. Asshole, she mutters. Some surprise. It's been what, a year?

Longer than that. Summer before last.

I'm sure Lillis Rae's been holding her breath. A goddamn surprise. That's a good one. She laughs and takes a long drag on the cigarette, watching his face.

I'm going to call her tomorrow, he says, softening his voice. First thing, I'll call in the morning, give her a heads-up. He holds up three fingers in a scout pledge. Promise.

What about tonight?

It's too late to call now. It's after midnight. She always hits the sack early. Ten-thirty—lights out. Like a goddamn Jesuit. It used to drive me crazy.

No, I mean, what about tonight? You got a room, or what? You planning on standing out here all night 'til some cowboy comes out and decides to fuck you up the ass?

Ah, come on, he says, reaching for her. What took so long in there? Did you score or are you just wasting time lecturing?

You should call her, she says. Only an asshole wouldn't call.

All right, so I'm an asshole, he says, spreading his arms. So fucking what? Who's the guy in the booth? I never seen him before.

A lot of shit has happened since you've been away, she says. A lot of shit. New people in, old people out. Moved on. Dead. Whatever. The guy's alright, but he's a total lech, always coming onto me when he knows I'm not into it anymore. I pay cash now, thank you.

What'd you score, anyway? Anything decent?

He gave me two pills—well, three—one for me, two for you. Dilaudids. He said you'd like them. You done these before?

She takes a foil packet from an inside pocket of her coat and hands it to him. I already took mine out, she says.

He opens the cigarette foil and examines the two tablets.

The yellow is the big one, she says, zipping her coat closed. Four mils, I think he said. The orange is two mils.

The Dilaudids look identical under the light.

They're morphine, Stace says. They'll dissolve easy in a fit.

He sold me the orange dillies for twenty apiece, the yellow was fifty, so that's what, fifty... ninety bucks.

You got a fit? he asks, folding the foil neatly around the two pills.

She purses her lips, blows a plume of smoke into his face. I might have one tucked away, she says. She is quite drunk, and suddenly starts shivering.

Let's go up to your room and party, Tanya, he says, remembering her name at that moment. He pulls her close, rubbing her back. The dope'll warm you up. We'll come back down for last call. I'll buy.

Fuck you, big spender, she says. I don't think so.

Come on. He pulls her toward him and she jerks back unsteadily, pushing his hand away from her waist. He takes her by the elbow. She tries to pry his fingers from her arm.

Let the fuck go of me, she says.

What is this shit? he says. Why are you so uptight?

Take your hands off. I gotta see Lillis Rae tomorrow night, for chrissakes. I'm gonna tell her I just fucked her husband? It's not like the old days anymore. I got some considerations to think about. And I'm working already, know what I mean? I don't want to screw things up with Bob. It's his room.

Gimme a fucking break, Stace says, letting her go. I remember Bob the Boyfriend, and he's a greasy sack of shit. You know the score: he's up at the oil field, probably fucking somebody else tonight. And it's only money between you, right? So keep his money but don't give me any loyalty bullshit because I don't buy it. You're beautiful and I want to fuck you tonight and that's not going to screw anything up between you and Bob. Besides, Lillis Rae is my ex, right? It's not like we've been living together for the past year and a half. So no biggie. You and me—two adults.

She taps her hand against the side of a car, the cherry of her cigarette flaring sparks.

Be nice, she says, looking up at him from beneath a frizz of blonde bangs. He's got money, which is more than you got.

Alright. Fuck. I'm sorry. Whatever you want. But get real, Tanya. You see him every month or so when he's on his way to the rigs, he puts you up in this motel, he fucks you and as many of your girlfriends as he can, and you're left right where you started. You still in that dump above the bakery? With the brown wallpaper?

He remembers Tanya's apartment: he and Lillis Rae had gone over to her place twice to drop off clothes or something, books maybe, and it was a place from the 1950s; hardwood floors and built-in cabinets and so on, okay except for the brown silk-type wallpaper in the living room, which made him depressed for some reason. It was like standing in a smoker's lung.

Suck me off, Tanya says. You're one to talk. You take out some scumbag and all of a sudden you're like Rambo or something. A real hard-ass. Right. She laughs and the laugh turns into a cough. Rambo with a hard-on. None of the rules apply to you anymore. The self-made man.

She shifts her purse around until it is between them, balances the fringed suede bag on a raised knee. He puts a hand under her thigh. She finds a half-empty plastic mickey of tequila in the bottom of the bag, opens it and drinks one-handed, the other hand resting in the small of his back.

At least Bob doesn't knock me around for his money. He's very nice to me. She swipes her mouth with the back of her wrist.

He's very nice to me, Stace mimics. He pulls out his wallet and tilts it so he can look into the billfold. He removes four twenties and a ten, folds them around a finger. Ninety bucks for the dillies, he says. He takes another pair of tens and a five and puts the money in Tanya's coat pocket. For you. Go down on me right now.

You're joking, right? Twenty-five bucks?

I'll pay for more later.

Damn right you will, but I'm not going down here. These are new jeans.

Tanya holds the bottle under her hand as she smokes, appraising him from behind the cigarette. She rolls her tongue over her teeth, sets the bottle on the hood of the car.

Alright, give me some of that tequila, he says. He takes a swallow from the bottle.

You're out of your fucking mind, she says, her breath alcohol and smoke.

Not yet I'm not, Stace says, running a hand over her coat. He pushes her back onto the hood of the car, sets the bottle down. She puts her heels up on the concrete planter, straddling him, touches the front of his jeans with the palm of her cigarette hand.

Not out here, you moron, she says. Sparks crawl over the back of her hand.

He opens her leather coat, bends to kiss the hollow of her throat.

Wait 'til we get inside. Bob's got friends around here, you know.

What's the room number?

Two-o-seven, she says. Up the stairs and to the left. Give me five minutes. I gotta make a call first.

Alright, he says. I'm cool. Up the stairs to the left.

I don't want them seeing you come in with me, she says. The night guy at the front desk is alright, but the manager is a prick, and I don't want him on my fucking case. Bob wants me to stay here for another week almost. It's Friday, right? So like, another eight days, 'til he finishes some contract.

Sure, he says. Five minutes. Who's the phone call for? A goodnight kiss for old Bob?

Ah shit. She pushes him off, stands again in the narrow aisle between the car and a muddy truck, stamps her feet as she stretches the jeans away from her thighs. What time is it?

No idea, he says. He pawned his watch, a good one he picked up somewhere, and hasn't had a chance to get another. It's for sure after midnight, he says.

Tanya squints at him through the smoke. I gotta get up early tomorrow, go home, pick up my mail, do laundry and do some shopping and shit before I see Lillis Rae. Know what I'm saying? I really feel like just going in and getting some sleep.

What time's your lesson? I'll drive you out to Lillis Rae's. That'd be absolutely no problem. No problem at all.

I don't think so. She hugs herself. No.

Kneel on my coat, he says. He unbuttons and shrugs out of the denim jacket, holds it out to her.

Asshole, she says. She puts the bottle down, takes the jacket, folds it into a pad. I'm fucking freezing my ass out here.

I heard you the second time, he says, touching the side of her neck with the tip of his finger. A tattoo or bruise, blue under her collarbone.

She takes a final drag of the cigarette and drops it beside the car.

Okay. She releases a lungful of smoke from the side of her mouth and kneels before him on the jacket. She unzips his jeans and slips her hand through the front of his underwear and runs her fingers between his legs, cupping his balls, her thumb on top of his cock. She pulls his cock through and leans forward, putting her lips to him. For a moment her lips are cold against his skin, and he realises it is as much the alcohol as the wind. He slides into her warm mouth, her tongue gliding down to the base of his cock, wrapping around him, and he hardens in her.

He holds her there, one hand warm beneath her hair, his fingers splayed on the back of her head.

Above the bar and the motor inn he can see the moon.

When he comes he bends over her head, holding her still, breath hissing out between his teeth, though he wanted to make no sound. He can feel cum, her saliva, running out from her mouth along the underside of his cock.

She rocks back on her heels, wipes the corners of her lips with her fingers, reaches up for the bottle of tequila. You been having too much salt, cowboy, she says. You should watch the heart attack. She rinses her mouth, spits.

He helps her to her feet and grabs his jacket. They both look down at his penis, small and wet, like a shrivelled amputee limb, and it shrinks as they watch until the grey head is barely visible in the fly of his jeans. He stretches it out and pisses against the front tire of the car, a fine spray of urine against his shins so that they both move back from the tire, his piss black on the rubber and silver in the arc between him and the car.

Let's go in now, Tanya says.

Got a smoke? he asks, and she lights one for herself and then one for him.

How do you like my truck? he asks, stopping at the red truck.

It's yours? She kicks the bumper, falling against him.

Not really, he says. Not really.

They move together unsteadily across the parking lot, their arms linked, her head against his shoulder. He cannot remember the last time he touched a woman.

MOTOR INN

STACE OPENS THE COURTYARD WINDOW and looks down at the indoor pool below. Maybe he should go for a swim in the morning. Sparks from his cigarette drift down and across the carpeted walkway and out through the handrailing. The water, lighted from below, is a strange chemical blue. Someone across the court is also smoking in a darkened window and he realises it is his own reflection.

He slides the window closed and turns. The bed has yellow sheets and pillowcases that do not match, a thin blanket with burn holes along the top where it has been folded down. He sits on the bed and uses the sheet to wipe his damp penis. He dresses, pulling his pants on slowly. His head is full of static, something moving slowly at the edges of the room. The grey television luminous.

He touches Tanya's shoulder through the sheet and she doesn't move. He takes her purse into the bathroom and turns on the light.

There is enough change in the bottom for a pack of rolling papers. He pockets her room card and goes out. The door locks. Down the stairs and out past the desk, the night clerk asleep with an earphone connecting him to the television behind the counter. A black and white shot of a woman in a bonnet and long dress, standing empty-handed in a stony field, sheep milling behind her.

Just down the access road a twenty-four hour service station is open, the tall sign buzzing and flickering like a faulty beacon. His neck feels hot and inflamed. With a thumb he traces two long scratches from just below his ear to his collarbone. He buttons his jacket all the way. He crosses under the fluorescent canopy and goes in, pays for the Zig-Zag papers and buys a postcard. The kid looks up from his magazine when Stace doesn't move away from the cash window.

Got a pen? Stace asks through the grille.

The kid pulls a pen out of a drawer and pushes it through the money slot.

Stace goes out with the pen and the kid shouts something behind the closing door. He walks back to the motor inn and lets himself into the silent room.

She is still under the sheet, her hair spread on the pillow.

He goes into the bathroom. Leaning forward, he stares into the mirror, stands with the light above the sink touching the top of his head until he feels like his head is burning. He takes the paper wrapper off a drinking glass, the glass clouded with scratches, fills it with her tequila. He lets the liquor back into his throat, feels the warm fumes through his nostrils, all around him quiet trumpets.

He has forgotten to buy a stamp. He dumps Tanya's purse onto the vanity. There is a stamp on a utility bill. He peels it off and wets the back against the lifted flap of the envelope until the stamp sticks to the card. He backward straddles the toilet and puts the card on the tank.

I told a friend all about you tonight.

He unwraps the remaining yellow Dilaudid and sets the open foil packet on the back of the toilet, pushes aside the purse clutter to find the syringe. It's a new one. With his teeth he rips open the plastic wrapper. He drops the pill into the chamber and adds water, shakes until the tablet dissolves. He takes the orange safety sheath off the needle, taps out the air, sets the fit down on the edge of the sink. In the pit of his stomach he can already feel the rush spread like a sweet nausea. He unsnaps his shirt and shrugs out of it, kicks off one of his boots to remove a sock. He pumps up his left arm and ties off with the sock, finds a good vein. Holding the twisted ends of the sock in his teeth, he steadies his arm on the corner of the vanity and shoots.

In the mirror he can see he is smiling. It's odd to see—he never smiles. Sometimes it feels like he's been pissed off about something his whole life. But not now. Everything blurs. Everything burns. Nothing can touch him now, everything is different.

He lays his forehead on the cold porcelain tank and hears the hiss of water filling secret chambers in the plumbing.

DICKEY

THERE WAS A MOUTH-SHAPED OIL STAIN on the pad of newspapers beneath the gun rack. Dickey must have cleaned the rifle recently and left it to drain, muzzle-down, against the wall. On the workbench, a soft rag had been used to wipe the barrel clean of excess oil. The rag was from an old pair of women's underwear, cotton speckled with faded pink and green in a design that would once have been floral.

Stace took the rifle down from the rack and unbuckled the shooting sling, neatly rolled the strap and dropped it on the workbench. He heard the Jeep grinding up the driveway and the Dobermans in the house went crazy. He snapped the loaded clip into place, knocking it with his fist until it locked with a solid click. He pulled the bolt back and chambered a round.

He closed the garage door and moved back in the dark until he felt the weight bench at the side of his leg and he sat down to wait with the 30.06 across his knees. Through the grimy side windows there was enough light to see cardboard boxes and tools piled along the workbench and the gleam of iron plates racked neatly at the weight machine.

He hoped the dogs would be left in the house. It would make what had to come next so much simpler.

The Jeep rattled to a stop outside the garage door and he heard the door creak open and the man shouted something to the dogs in the house and they shut up at once.

A key rasped in the lock and a crack of light appeared at the bottom of the roll-up door, and Stace saw Dickey's thongs and his bare legs and then the door slid all the way up and the man was looking right at him.

What the fuck, Dickey said, and Stace saw his arms tense and his face go still, his arms up over his head, still holding onto the garage door, like he was surrendering.

What the fuck, Dickey said again, and swallowed, getting his voice back. What the fuck are you doing here?

Stace got to his feet and the man backed away a step from the garage door, dropping his arms to his side, shifting his weight like he was going to run for it. He was a little guy, wearing a T-shirt with the emblem of a distillery on it, sweat pants he'd hacked-off into shorts.

Hey, Dickey, Stace said quietly.

What's it about? What's it about? The little man backed toward the Jeep, which was still idling. His eyes jumped around, all over Stace, around the yard.

Stace's hands were sweating inside the tan garden gloves, his shirt sticking to the small of his back.

Whatever you want, you got the wrong guy, know what I'm saying? The wrong guy. Dickey looked around but there was nowhere to go. His face was glazed, ashen, his hands closed tight around something invisible. He was about an arm's length from the front of the Jeep.

Stace released the safety. He could hear the dogs whining now from inside the house.

Don't do this, Dickey said. It's not worth it. He spat in the dirt, wiped his forehead with the side of his wrist, shaded his eyes against the glare of the yard to look in at Stace.

Did Steve send you here? he asked. Steve and me cut a deal. We cut a deal and worked things out, no problem. Everything is cool, right? I got cash in the basement of the house.

Stace could see it all slowed down, like in a movie. Everything slow and carefully done so he could concentrate on the last few moments, the details, before it would all speed up and get jerky and he wasn't sure how it was going to happen.

Come into the garage, Stace said, and stepped back with the rifle. Dickey squatted and reached under the Jeep and flung something at Stace, an empty beer bottle. It spun off Stace's shoulder, knocked to the garage floor without breaking.

The dogs started going apeshit again.

Stace stepped toward the front of the garage and Dickey rolled, jumped to his feet, not more than a dozen feet away, looking at Stace. Stace brought the rifle up toward his shoulder. Dickey's chest floated before him. He squeezed the trigger and the butt of the rifle slammed back hard against him, the ejected shell casing a blur. Blind, the black flocculent, dissolving, then the green afterimage of the muzzle flash printed negative on his retinas. He was deaf in his right ear for five minutes.

*   *   *

The yard was empty. Dickey knocked down like he stepped into a hole.

Stace lowered the rifle and his shoulder ached from the kick of the recoil pad. He took the clip off and laid the rifle on the workbench and found the shell casing where it had rolled beneath the bench, and he noticed his hands were shaking. Leave me, he thought, and when the shaking stopped at last and lifted off him he didn't know how much time had passed. Perhaps only a minute. He grabbed a knife and a roll of plastic sheeting he'd found with the hunting gear in the garage and went out into the yard.

It was late afternoon, June, the poplar tree's sweet green breath above the garage. It was snowing. Stace looked up and could see only white cotton drifting down from the tree into the light. Dickey was face down, the hair on the back of his head riffling in the breeze. Stace knelt beside him and he could smell a mist of blood in the air. At that moment he was not doing anything but thinking. He didn't know what he was thinking. Bright arterial blood was pumping from the exit wound in Dickey's back, fragments of bone and tissue at the mouth of the wound, the T-shirt soaked through with blood. He could have put three fingers into the hole. Stace unfolded the plastic and laid it out like a sheet and rolled Dickey over onto it. There was a tiny dimple in the front of the T-shirt where it had been driven into Dickey's chest by the bullet. Around the pucker a small spreading ring of red. Dickey looked up at Stace with his mouth open. Cotton fluff was falling on his damp face and sticking.

Dickey said, My dogs. Stace bent down with his ear to the man's mouth. What did you say? Stace asked. I'm shot, Dickey whispered. There was blood on his teeth where he had bitten through his lip. The veins in his neck were corded with effort, his fingers jerking on the plastic. He stared up at Stace and there was something Stace should have done but he couldn't figure it out.

The cicadas started buzzing again, a high electric sound that faltered and then came on strong from all around. Stace put his gloved hand on the bumper of the Jeep and pulled himself to his feet. He walked around to the driver's door and reached in to shut off the engine. There was a kid on the passenger side, strapped into a carrier seat, the child's face shiny with tears. He turned the key and the Jeep went quiet. The kid blinked at him, pudgy fingers in its mouth.

In the shade of the garage, Stace leaned against the warm flank of the Jeep, closed his eyes and listened to the dogs barking wildly in the empty house.

THREE IN THE MORNING

When Stace awakes his hand is on fire. Blue alcohol flames along his arm.

He tries to roll over and something is wrong with his elbow because it will not bend properly and when he tries to sit up he finds he cannot. He lies without moving and there is something cold behind his neck and he realises he is blind.

Above him the rustle of clothing, a shadow, the smell of aftershave.

Jesus fuck. Get in here, Tanya, a man's voice calls above him.

White. His eyes are wide open and he sees only white.

Stace tries to turn his head. He is on the floor looking up at the underside of the toilet tank. A chrome inlet pipe beaded with condensation. The clear plastic oval of the shut-off valve.

It's porcelain at the back of his neck; he's lying with his head against the wall between the toilet and the tub. Stace feels with his tongue a loose tooth. The coppery tang of blood in his mouth, bitter vomit.

The light is blinding, he cannot close his eyes, he aches all over. His arm is burning but he cannot move, can't feel anything but a fatigue as deep as bone.

Wake up, fuckhead!

The man is shaking Stace roughly with one hand, holding onto the sink for support.

Come on. Get your ass up, the man says.

Stace is staring at a pair of snakeskin boots with worked silver toe caps, a frayed jean cuff. Stace tries to move, cannot.

You're fucking out of here, asshole, the man says. He grabs Stace by the hair and lifts his head off the bathroom floor. There is no resistance.

He lowers Stace's head to the floor, kneels beside the toilet to place his fingers to the side of Stace's throat.

The man rocks back on his heels and pulls Stace over onto his side. Stace's eyes are sightless and dry in their sockets, his face sunken and hollow.

Come in here, Tanya, the man says.

Tanya comes into the bathroom and sets a canvas bag on the floor, squats beside the man.

It wasn't my fault, Wes, she says. For God's sake, it wasn't my fault.

What the fuck is this shit? The man, Wes, holds up the syringe. What kind of shit'd this asshole do tonight?

I picked up some pills, I told you. Dilaudid. We each popped a small one after we fucked, then I fell asleep. That was around one or two — I was wiped. I thought he was maybe saving the big one for some other time. I don't know. I didn't know he was going to shake and bake. He asked me earlier if I had a rig, but he didn't mention it again. I was sleeping.

Looks like this asshole did more than that, Wes says. It smells like he downed a forty pounder of tequila before he got to the dillies.

He drops the syringe into the sink. Clean this shit up but don't throw it in the waste basket. Get a separate bag. And wipe up his puke. It's making me heave.

What about an antidote? she asks. Hit him with adrenaline or something. She fumbles with the bag, and it seems she is crying.

It's about two hours too late for fucking Narcan. I don't have it, anyway. Wes rocks back on his boot heels and steeples the tips of his fingers, thinking.

He's drunk, Tanya says. Just drunk and passed out, aren't you, baby? She kneels and touches her fingers lightly to Stace's face. He's sound asleep, she says, brushing her hair back from her eyes, half-turning up to Wes.

Quit it, Wes says, gripping her hand. He's not fucking sleeping. He's not going to wake up.

That's not true, Tanya says.

You gotta get him the fuck out of here, Wes says. Get his arms, I'll take his legs.

Awkwardly, they move him away from the tub, the buckle of Stace's belt scraping across the floor. His body sags between them. They heave him up and drop him face down on the bed. The whites of Stace's eyes glaring sightlessly into the burn holes of the blanket.

Tanya squats, closes his left eye. She runs her finger down Stace's naked back, following the curve of spine, brings her finger up to her nose. Touches the tip of her finger to her tongue. He's wet, he's covered in some sort of jelly. She puts her hand out again to Stace's face.

It's honey, she says. It tastes just like honey, Wes. He's covered in honey. Taste it, she says, extending her finger toward Wes.

Wes leans forward from the edge of the bed, sniffs the cloudy viscous liquid on her finger.

Tanya pushes her hair behind her ear, lowers her mouth to Stace's skin.

Get the fuck off him. Wes shakes her roughly. You're freaking me out.

I can feel him inside there, she says, her ear to Stace's chest. It's very faint. He's alive.

He's got no pulse, Wes says.

It's sweet, she says. It's not quite honey, it's like that royal jelly shit. She moves her tongue down Stace's back, shifting her legs until she is kneeling over the prostrate figure, hair hanging down around her face. She looks up at Wes. Taste him, she says. Come on.

The bed creaks. Wes touches Stace's shoulder with the tip of a finger, as if afraid now he will wake him. He licks his finger. I've tasted this somewhere before, he says.

Where? she asks. She tilts her head up, grins at Wes. Her face is wet, shining. Hair clings to her cheeks, the curve of her jaw.

You're one fucked-up bitch, Wes says.

I want to eat him, Tanya says. I want to fuck him.

What is this shit? Some kind of aphrodisiac?

If his sweat tastes like honey imagine what his cum tastes like.

She gets up and slides her jeans off, straddles Stace's back.

Are you seriously gonna fuck him?

Tanya strips off her top and drops it onto the bed.

Wes glides his hand down over the roundness of her ass.

She lowers her mouth to Stace's skin once again, tracing scars with her tongue.

Wes kneels in behind Tanya, moving his hands down around the thrust of hipbones and across the soft curve of her abdomen. The chalk glow of her skin. She sways side to side, letting her nipples brush across the cool skin of the dead man. Wes pushes a finger into her from behind.

You're wet, he says, his mouth close to her ear.

Get his pants off, Tanya says.

Wes reaches down between her knees, grabbing Stace roughly by the hips.

Take his shoulders and flip him with me, Wes says. Together they turn Stace onto his back. Stace's head lolls to the side, his mouth partly open. She bends down, kisses Stace's lips. There's honey in his mouth, she says.

Wes unbuckles Stace's belt, tugs at his jeans.

Tanya lowers herself until she is lying full-length on Stace.

His skin is cool, she says. Maybe his spirit is travelling on another plane. She kisses Stace's mouth, pushing her tongue in between his teeth, into honeyed darkness beneath his tongue.

Wes rubs his bristly chin against Tanya's ass, sliding one hand between her legs, his forefinger hooking up and into her, bringing wetness up to her clitoris as his other hand strokes the inside of her thighs. She lifts her pelvis, pushing Wes's hand away from her thighs.

I don't need you, she says. I don't need you now. She sits up across Stace's hips, touches his penis. His dick's hard, she says. She pulls Stace's penis toward her, pushes the head gently inside. With her free hand she touches Stace's balls, the thick vein at the base of his cock.

Wes kisses her neck, shoulders, his hands moving over her body. Her nipples are hard in the cool room.

She lowers herself onto Stace, guiding his penis into her, begins fucking him under the steadying pressure of Wes's hands on her hips.

You're making love to a dead man, Wes says in her ear.

Tanya's eyes are closed: she is working toward something Wes cannot see.

STRIP

HE IS LYING naked on the bed. Behind him he can hear Wes's voice, angry, then Tanya. In the mirror, they are standing together, looking down at him curled on the bed.

I don't fucking know, Wes. I don't fucking know. Tanya's voice, exhausted.

Let me see his wallet, Wes says.

It's by the coffee-maker on the table, Tanya replies, sitting on the bed next to Stace. The creak of bedsprings. She is wearing her leather coat and no pants and she is shivering. She rocks forward, elbows on her bare knees, buries her face in her hands. Her hair is pulled back with a velvet scrunchy and she looks ten years older.

Wes rifles through Stace's wallet.

Credit cards? A bank card? We can't touch those. He drops the cards to the table. A pawnshop receipt for some piece-of-crap Seiko watch? Fuck off. His driver's licence—we could sell that. No, we fucking can't use that; we've got to trash all this shit. A video rental card, fuck! I don't believe this. Twenty-five bucks?

Wes slaps the wallet on the table. Where's the money he fronted for the drugs?

It's in my purse, Tanya mumbles between her hands. But it's only like ninety bucks. I told you he only bought three dilaudid.

Give it here.

Fuck you! She raises her head, glaring at Wes.

Give it.

Fuck you. That's my goddamn money. I asked you here to help me, not fucking rip me off.

It's not in your purse, Wes says. There's about enough money in here to make a phone call to Bob. I'm sure he'd love to hear what you've been doing tonight. Where's the money from Bob? Where's your fucking paycheque from Bob? Wes flings her purse across the room. It crashes against the bathroom door: coins, lipstick, cigarettes, coupons, envelopes, an empty plastic mickey scatter across the floor.

Silence, then Tanya says, It's in my stash. All the money's in my stash.

How much, Tanya? Do you want me to help out or not? 'Cause I can walk out of here right now and forget I saw any of this mess. I can drive back to the city and maybe get a few more hours of shut-eye before morning, know what I'm saying? Easy. Just walk out.

Four hundred thirty, four-eighty maybe. Including the money he paid me back for the dillies.

I want half. Two-forty and I'll get rid of him. Two-forty. That's about two hours of some dickhead lawyer's time. You do the math. That's what it's going to cost to have me clean up this mess for you.

Wes!

Hey, don't Wes me, fuck-up. You got a major problem here, Tanya. You got what, six hours or so before housekeeping comes in here to clean the bathroom? If our friend here doesn't decide to wake up at check-out time, the maid's going to find Mr. Fucking Bugeyes lying beside the tub with his fucking tongue hanging out of his mouth. She tells security, security calls the cops, and if you wait for the cops to haul a stiff out of this room it's going to cost more than two hundred forty bucks for lawyers, I kid you not. And then there's Bob to think about. Bob and his wife. You and fat Bob've had it pretty quiet here up 'til now, nice and cozy, but see what I'm getting at? Say goodbye to Bob and his bankroll, say hello to waitressing. You're too old to peel anymore. Or maybe you want to be a seatcover for those truckers down in the café. You following me or am I going too fast for you?

Tanya mutters something that does not carry, drops her head into her hands again.

Wes squats in front of her, a hand on her knee.

I'm laying out your options here, Tanya, in the clearest way I can. I'll make this my problem but it's going to cost you two hundred forty bucks. That's fucking cheap, for what I'm doing here for you tonight. Cheap.

What about the wallet? she asks, reaching for her jeans.

Take the bank cards and the driver's licence and the video card and cut them into little slivers. So there's no numbers together. You got something to cut with?

No.

Wes unsnaps a leather holster on his belt and takes out a knife, opens a scissors blade, hands the knife to Tanya.

Chop chop, he says.

*   *   *

Wes paces the strip of carpet between bed and television, looking down at Stace's still body.

We gotta get this fuck dressed and out of here quick, he says, mostly to himself. We carry him out like he's totally wasted, the two of us, prop him up between us. Either that or we need a big fucking bag, like a hockey bag, and some rope or straps. You got anything in your car? A tool kit or something?

No, Tanya says. A blanket, I think. I got a blanket. She is hunched at the table, clipping Stace's cards into an ashtray.

Shit, we gotta carry him out before he's stiff as a fucking board. Wes picks up Stace's arm, pumps it twice. Feel him, he says. Rigor mortis.

Tanya reaches around, touches Stace's hand. I seen where you gotta break legs or arms to bend them once they stiffen up like that.

Don't tell me what I already know, Wes says, dropping the arm back. He adjusts his baseball cap, looking over Tanya's shoulder to check her work on the cards. This has to be thought through carefully, he says.

You want coffee? Tanya asks. Maybe that'll help. I'm fucking wiped. She tears open a foil packet of coffee and dumps it into the basket of the coffee-maker, plugs it into the wall beside the TV. The coffee-maker hisses, draws a gurgling breath of air.

Wes picks up a lit cigarette from the edge of the table, drags twice, hands the cigarette back to Tanya. He paces, letting smoke out slowly through his nostrils.

We'll dress him, then we'll go out to the parking lot and get his truck. He's parked near the bar, so I'll walk to his truck. You get the blanket from your car and wait at the side exit and I'll bring the truck around and park it right at the door. We'll come back up here and get him, kind of carry him between us like he can't walk. He's passed out, it's Friday night, nothing unusual in that. We drape the blanket over him in case we pass anyone in the hallway, and we go down together to the truck. If no one sees us, if it's all clear, we put him in the truck on the passenger seat. Is this making sense? We throw the blanket over him like he's gone to sleep there. Like I'm driving my buddy home after a bender. Very nice, very thoughtful. You take my keys and follow me in my car out to the reservoir. No one's out there this time of the night. We ditch him with the truck somewhere on a logging road and no one'll find him for days.

He twitches aside the drapes, looks out into the blue courtyard.

Get the rig from the bathroom, and don't forget his boots and the sock, he says, letting the curtains fall as he turns from the window.

We'll put the rig on the seat of the truck beside him, the mickey on the floor — we lay it all out so the cops can see it clear. It'll look to them like some asshole got pissed, drove his truck out to the reservoir, spiked himself and passed out, ODed and froze to death, got a bubble in his vein, whatever. And by the time they find him in a day or two, no one is going to be able to figure out what the fuck killed him. Right? Who gives a shit how he bit it? We've laid it all right there under their noses. We make it easy for them. Okay…? So after we ditch him, we drive back in my car, I drop you back here at the room, you try to get some sleep. Go for breakfast or whatever. Clean up the bathroom and try to get rid of the puke smell. Do your thing tomorrow like usual. If you stay calm everything'll go down fine. No one saw you leave the bar with this guy, that was good, that's in our favour, no one saw you come up to the room together, no one sees you leave with him. You're fucking clean. Clean.

Tanya hands him a cup of coffee, passes the cigarette. Wes sits on the corner of the table with his boots on the bed, stares down at Stace, the cigarette burning between his fingers.

Funny you should mention the reservoir, Tanya says. I found this in the bathroom. She slides the postcard out from under the phone directory and flips it over. He must've wrote it tonight, after I was asleep.

Wes takes the postcard, reads it quickly.

It sounds like a suicide note, she says.

Steve should see this, Wes says. He flexes the card between his fingers, is silent a moment, thinking.

Tanya retrieves the cigarette, taps a finger of ash onto the credit card debris. Why the fuck else would Stace have disappeared, right? I always figured he had something to do with Dickey. He just walked away from Lillis Rae and vanished and no one could find Dickey all of a sudden?

Steve'll flip, Wes says. It drove him crazy, trying to figure out what the christ happened to Dickey. His kid left out there at the reservoir but all the dope money gone? A boating accident? Steve never bought it. It just didn't make sense.

Accidents happen, Tanya says. How many people fall out of boats every year?

Wes reads the postcard again, flips it over to pick at the loose stamp.

He was scared of Steve, Tanya says. He panicked and took the money and then there was no way back. He told me a bit about it tonight in the bar. It was eating him up and he wanted to talk. He wanted to come back and he needed to talk it through.

What else did he say? What happened to the cash? He blow it all?

I tried not to listen. I don't need to know that shit.

And the body? What'd he use, concrete boots? Dickey never floated. If he was in the reservoir he would've floated eventually. You can't keep a body down. Somebody would've found him.

Stace tied cinder blocks on him, she says. Three cinder blocks.

Mystery number two hundred and three solved, Wes says, looking at the postcard. So Dickey went for a swim and the cash floated away. Bye bye Dickey, bye bye.

The poor kid, is what I always think, Tanya says. Dickey was an asshole, but he loved the kid.

He's not the only kid in the world to grow up without an old man, Wes says.

He's probably lucky. Tanya rubs out the cigarette.

Wes taps the postcard against his thigh, blows across the top of the coffee. Sometimes it's hard to know what to do, isn't it? he asks. Fucking hard. Much as I'd like to, I don't think we can show this to Steve. We can tell Steve what happened to Dickey, but we gotta leave the card on Stace. This totally looks like a suicide note. If the cops find it on Stace, it'll make it that much easier for them to take it as an accidental or intentional OD and not look any further. It simplifies our lives and the cops get to close Dickey's case. Even Steve's happy in the end. It's his drugs in Stace's veins. Karma. Payback time.

You think this'll work out, Wes?

Yes. Everything'll be fine. It's a fuck-up but it's going to be okay.

Wes drops his feet off the bed and crosses the room, picks up Stace's shirt from the bathroom floor. He slides the postcard into the breast pocket.

Time to rock and roll, he says.

*   *   *

Wes shrugs into his coat and takes the magnet box with the truck keys from the table.

Tanya laces her boots and puts her purse together. Ready, she says, zipping her coat.

Wes listens at the door, puts his eye to the peephole. It's clear, he says. He motions Tanya forward and opens the door and she switches the light off as they slip out of the room to the walkway. Above the bed, the white globe glows an instant and then dissolves in darkness.

As the door closes behind them, Stace notices for the first time the man sitting silently in the armchair by the door.

HOOD

IT'S ABOUT TIME, the man says. I wasn't sure when you were coming through. His voice is gravelly and low.

He levers himself up from the armchair, an old man but powerful. He is wearing a grey sweatshirt and dark pants, almost invisible in the dim room but for his hair, a shock of unkempt silver.

The man picks up a nylon tote bag and crosses the room, a slow exhalation of minty breath as he lowers himself to sit on the corner of the bed. He is sucking on a peppermint. The candy clicks against his teeth when he talks.

The snap of a lighter, the hiss of flame. You can feel this, can't you? A cold tongue of flame against Stace's face now, the smell of scorching hair.

Stace tries to move, lift his face away, but the man pushes his head to the mattress. Stace can smell Tanya's perfume, her hair, on the sheets.

Just checking, the man growls, putting the lighter away. I think you're ready. Your strength is coming back. Now we can go.

The man's low voice beside him, a dark shape between him and the window. Hands under his arms, breath along his cheek.

Up.

Stace is standing in the dim room and the man has an arm around his waist and is half carrying him on a hip. Blood sinks from Stace's head and the room dissolves in floating black spots.

Come on. Put your arm around my waist, the man says, picking up the nylon bag with his free hand. It'll be easier.

It is too much of an effort to resist. Stace staggers forward and slides one foot in front of the other, bumping the edge of the mattress with his knees. His legs feel alien, dislocated. They shuffle together along the side of the bed, the man holding Stace upright.

Easy, he says. Easy. A sandpapery, callused hand clutching Stace's naked shoulder.

Stace closes his eyes and leans against the man, his head roaring. The man steadies himself on the corner of the table, opens the door. They move around the edge of the door and out into the walkway and then slowly along the handrail to the elevator, the pool swaying chlorine-blue below them.

They go down. Stace can barely stand and the lights in the mirrored elevator are so bright they hurt his eyes. The elevator stops at the lobby and his knees buckle and the man jams him into the corner of the elevator to keep him upright.

This way.

They cross the flare of the lobby and go out the doors. The pavement is freezing beneath Stace's bare feet, his penis and scrotum swaying against his naked thighs. They walk out through darkness and Stace can see again, away from the light.

Stop.

The scrape of keys. The man opens a door and helps him up into a vehicle, a panel van, the vinyl seat ice cold against his naked buttocks. The door closes beside him and he can feel wind buffet the van. The man climbs in the other side and slams his door.

Look at them, the man commands. He taps his side window with a finger.

Wes is parking the red truck. Tanya is standing in the lighted doorway at the side of the motor inn, looking out at Wes. She has a blanket balled up in her arms.

The man laughs and turns the key in the van's ignition.

It's a fucked up world, isn't it, son?

The steel door closes behind Wes and the parking lot is deserted again.

The man backs the van out and they pull around the corner of the motor inn, stop next to the red pickup. The man gets out of the van and walks around the driver's side of the truck and leans in to release the hood and then opens the hood and reaches into the engine and does something before dropping the hood and pressing it closed. He gets back into the van. They wait.

A few minutes pass and then the steel door bangs open and Tanya sticks her head out, looks around.

There you be, the man says. Your grand exit.

He reaches into the nylon bag and takes out a Polaroid camera and a notebook. A souvenir for you, he says to Stace. He rolls down his window and pokes the camera out.

Wes and Tanya push backward through the door, between them a figure with a blanket over its head, legs sagging uselessly.

The camera flashes and a print slides out the front of the camera. The man sets the camera on the console between their seats and puts the print inside his sweatshirt, counts for a minute to warm it and then removes the polaroid and peels it open. What do you think? he asks. He looks at the print and then jots something down on the bottom with a pen. He opens the notebook and writes quickly, glances at his watch, paperclips the photograph to the entry in the book. The book is jammed with polaroids, the spine bulging, the whole thing held together with a thick rubber band.

Stace drops back and feels the metal door frame beside his head. He closes his eyes and when he opens them again the van is on a highway, a yellow divider line flicking under the headlights. The man is humming something, a forefinger keeping time above the steering wheel. He glances at Stace, reaches across the dash and flicks the dial on a police scanner. A voice filters sideways through static, unintelligible.

Mint? the man asks. The ashtray is filled with round white peppermints.

Stace lifts away from the door frame but his head pounds and he sinks back silent.

My name's Emmett, the man says, studying Stace in the dim light of the dashboard. I'm here to take care of you.

He is maybe sixty, but Stace can't say for sure. There are hard knots of muscle along the man's jaw, deep weathered creases cutting down from the sides of his mouth as if he has spent too much time working outdoors. His forearms ropy with muscle, a blurry tattoo like a sailor where the sleeves of the sweatshirt have been bunched above his wrists.

The van slows, turns across the highway onto a side road and comes to a stop in absolute darkness. Emmett kills the engine, the interior of the van lit only by the green glow of the scanner's display. Wind slams the van. He runs fingers through his silver hair, scrubs his face with empty hands, yawns widely.

Headlights approach, a tow truck with a rack of running lights across the top of the cab. Hooked to the tow-cable pulley is a long yellow car, the front of the Lincoln Continental winched up under the boom lights, the grille dripping muddy weeds. The truck pulls to a stop level with the van and both drivers roll their windows down.

How did it go? Emmett asks, leaning on a forearm out his window. His breath a white cloud dispersing.

I got her out of the reservoir, the tow truck driver says. What a bitch.

I took the kids in already. I'm on my way back now, last pick-up for the night, I hope.

Fucking kids. The tow truck driver holds up a hand and the truck rolls slowly past them, the yellow car gliding away into darkness.

Fucking kids, Emmett mutters to himself, reaching up to turn on the interior light. He twists around in his seat and squeezes past Stace to the rear of the van. Bench seats coiled with wet ropes, muddy footprints on the metal floor, a pair of sodden jeans hanging black and dripping and empty from a hook. Emmett pulls a bundle of white canvas from a mesh holder behind his seat.

Put these on, he says. He drops a wrinkled pair of white cotton coveralls into Stace's lap.

Stace stares down at the bundle, cold on his naked thighs.

Come on, Emmett urges.

Stace, seated, searches in the dark for an armhole or leghole, jams his feet through the legs of the coveralls.

Emmett clambers back into the driver's seat, watches Stace dress.

Stace pulls on the coveralls and hitches the outfit up over his shoulders, awkward in the cramped seat. The coveralls smell of wood smoke.

And your boots, Emmett says. They're under your seat.

He slides his bare feet into the hiking boots without lacing them.

Emmett reaches across to Stace and pulls the zipper at the neck of the coveralls, bringing up a long cowl like a hood over Stace's face, blinding him. Stace panics, raises an arm weakly to the hood, and Emmett grabs his wrist and holds him.

It's just a temporary measure, Emmett assures him as he fastens the hood. It's not a long drive. Sleep. Put your head back. You're going to need your strength.

Emmett rolls up his window and starts the van.

Stace's breathing racketing inside the hood, cotton humid on his mouth and nose.

LIVING ROOM

STACE TOUCHED HER FACE with the back of his fingers.

I hate you, Lillis Rae said. She was looking right into his eyes and he had to close his eyes to shut her out.

It was the last time they made love. The room was filled with late afternoon sunlight and through the open windows they could hear the purple martins calling out over the hot lawn.

He worked his fingers into her neck, the muscles of her shoulders, her shirt sliding and bunching beneath his hands.

I thought I knew what you did, what you were capable of, where you stood, but I don't, she said. Whatever it is you've done, I don't want to know. There are others who know more about you than I do, now.

He worked down under the muscles, moving in slow deep semicircles, his thumbs at the base of her neck, the warm velvety skin supple beneath his thumbs, working out from her spine, his fingers under her arms.

He pulled the bottom of her shirt out from her jeans.

This is not a good idea, she said.

Why not?

You know why.

He took off her earrings, put them on the coffee table. Tell me why.

He put a hand under her shirt, to her belly, pushed her down until she was lying on the couch with her head on the armrest. She swung her legs up and into his lap. He took her shoes off, ran his fingers around her cool, bony ankles. Tell me why.

It's because I love you and I don't know why else. To see it all destroyed by one stupid thing…. She waved her hand in the air. She closed her eyes.

Stace picked up one of her feet, laid his warm cheek against the sole of her foot, cupping her heel in his hand.

That feels nice, she said.

They waited in silence awhile. The only movement, his thumb stroking the smooth arch of her foot. He was losing it all, everything, he knew that. If there had been a way out he would have taken it but there wasn't. It was now someone else's living room, someone else's furniture. So this is my heart breaking, he thought, looking down at her.

Do you mind if I take my shirt off?

He pressed his lips to the underside of her toes.

Her breasts were small and flat to her chest, the nipples like ornaments dark and high on her body. He shifted on the couch and knelt between her legs to undo her belt. She braced her feet and arched her back so he could get the jeans down. The delicate bones of her chest spreading like bird's wings.

I don't know what the hell I'm doing, she said suddenly.

Yes you do, he replied.

He pulled the jeans off, leaving her naked legs around him.

Let me just look at you for a while, he said.

She locked her ankles behind his neck and pulled him down. He kissed her breasts while she unbuttoned his pants, hooked the waistband with her long toes. Help me, she said.

He went partway in.

Her lips moved across his cheek. I think this is a very bad idea, she said into his ear.

He was inside her deeply, her thighs around his waist, her head coming up now against his neck.

You're so far away already, she whispered. Where are you?

He balanced himself with the top of his head in the hollow of her shoulder and with both hands lifted her ass off the cushions, his fingers sliding around and into her.

What are we going to do? Lillis Rae asked.

He breathed through his mouth so that he would not cry, his throat clamped as if by an iron band, and he saw that she was waiting for an answer and he said nothing, nothing, holding her against his chest. He knew it was over and she knew it too and was waiting for him to say it, say anything, but he could not shape an answer, even a single word.

He was twenty-eight years old and he reached down inside himself for something he knew should be there and from the kitchen he could hear the kid calling for Dickey, calling for his father who was not there and never would be.

SATURDAY MORNING EARLY 2

LODGE

THE VAN SLOWS, turns off the road they have been travelling on, swaying in ruts, the engine in low as it goes up an incline. Loose gravel rattling up around the wheel wells and down the length of the underbed as Emmett wrestles the wheel and they climb until the road levels and they come finally to a stop. Silence. It is maybe an hour later, he cannot tell. Stace waits open-eyed and numb under the cotton hood.

Emmett gets out and slams his door, walks around to open Stace's side.

He unfastens the hood. We can take it off now, he says. Emmett unzips the top of the coveralls and the hood falls open. Stace shakes his head to clear it. He feels stronger and steadier, alert.

Let's go, Emmett says.

Stace gets down from the van and he sees ahead a low building set back under a seething murmur of inky trees, two windows throwing blocks of light out across the ground. A string of feeble lights overhead sways in a gust of wind. He shivers in the mountain air, smells pine and wood smoke and snow.

They walk together across a gravel lot and up two wooden steps and across a porch, Emmett's hand on the back of his neck. A heavy door is opened and they go inside.

To the right, Emmett says.

There is the sound of many voices. They go through another door and they are in a long, crowded hall, log beams rising overhead to a peaked roof. At the far end, a soot-blackened hearth. The door swings closed behind them and the room falls silent a moment, people twisting in their seats to look toward them in the doorway, and the hum of conversation comes up again. It looks like the TV lounge in a hospital. Maybe fifty people of all ages sit at scarred plywood cafeteria tables, playing cards or reading books. In ratty sofas by the fireplace, others rest with sweaters draped over their faces.

Emmett guides Stace across the room, down an aisle between haphazard tables, into a roped-off area of wall booths segregated from the rest of the room by a red velvet cord stretched between stanchions. Stace bangs his knees as Emmett pushes him to sit at a table.

Wait here, Emmett says.

He is sitting at a small, brightly lit table across from a woman. The woman stares into the steamed window, wipes her hand across the glass so she can see outside into the night. Sees only her own smeared reflection in the dark.

Hey, Stace says across the table.

The woman turns away from the window, startled almost, looks at him. Blood has soaked the front of her coveralls, across her forehead a wide, fresh gash.

Behind her, the main door opens, and the woman twists around in her seat to look back. A fat man coming through the door catches her eye and grimaces as he shakes his head. He comes to the booth, slides onto the bench beside the woman. Ice is beaded on the cuffs of his pants and sleeves. The lapels of his coveralls are wet, hair slick across his skull, a smear of blood on his cheek.

The woman pulls him close, using her thumb to wipe the blood away. There's blood on your face, she says. He puts his hands on the table, looking away from her. His fingers are red from the cold.

Did you see anything? she asks.

The man shakes his head. No. Not a sign. We're in the middle of a goddamn wasteland. Not even a road except the one we came up on. I could only follow that about a quarter mile before I had to turn back. No lights, no nothing. I didn't want to get lost out there.

The fat man is staring at the woman's throat, a lock of hair falling across his eye.

Is it still bleeding? he asks. Breath whistles out his nostrils.

No. It's stopped, the woman says.

I'm Chaz. The man extends a meaty red hand across the table to Stace. This is my wife, Linda, he says, hooking a thumb at the woman. When did you get in?

Stace shrugs. I don't know.

He came in about five, ten minutes ago, Linda offers.

Did he? We've been here I don't know, a couple hours anyway, and not a blasted sign what's going on, what we're waiting for.

They brought us here with hoods on, the woman says. We couldn't see a thing.

I came in a van, Stace says.

There's no van out front, Chaz says. He came in just now?

Linda nods.

I didn't see nothing. Maybe I was around the backass side of this damn building.

Why are we here? Stace asks.

We had an accident, Linda says. We went off the road. Now we're waiting.

There was another guy, he was really torn to shit, they took him out of here an hour ago. Chaz puts his hands on the table, leans toward Stace. His clothes was all soaked in blood. Looked like somebody shot him in the head. A young negro boy. They had him lying on the floor by the door there. Chaz points over his shoulder. There was two of them attendants had to carry him in.

Stace looks around. At a booth near the back a group of kids are talking excitedly. Their faces are puffy, mysteriously pallid, their clothes soaking wet. Some of them have taken their shoes off and their jackets off and spread wet clothing on a vacant table.

It is an old lodge, a long, high-ceilinged room with wainscoting and paneled walls. Fluorescent lights in dusty yellowed fixtures run the length of the room. An abandoned ping-pong table in one corner.

I had a hood on my head, Stace says to the man and the woman. I didn't see where we came. I don't even know how long we drove to get here.

What happened to you? Linda asks.

Stace shrugs. I woke up and I was lying on the bathroom floor. I guess I passed out. The old guy who brought me in here— Emmett—was sitting in a chair by the door, watching me lie there.

Shitty. At least you didn't see it coming, Chaz says. I could see it coming and I was trying to pull out of the slide but nothing was grabbing, we were just drifting right into the guard rail, then *boom*—Chaz brings his palms together and skids one off the other—a road sign goes crack over the windshield and we're into the ditch. Must've took about three seconds total.

We blacked out for a bit, I think, Linda continues. When we woke up there were two people, a man and a woman, pulling us out. We were upside down in the ditch. At first we thought they were maybe helping us. We were wet. There was blood everywhere but I wasn't worried. They got us out through the windshield and up onto the road and then they got us out of our wet clothes and put us in these hooded coveralls. They put us in the van and zipped us up, and drove us here.

The weird thing, Chaz says, lowering his voice, is that I recognised the guy who pulled us out of the wreck. I know him. I *know* him. I can't remember his name, but I'd swear it was a guy who used to work construction with me about twenty years ago—big tall guy who used to shoot pool way back with some league. Now, I ain't never been into voodoo stuff, know what I'm saying, but I heard he killed himself when his wife left him for some other guy.

You didn't see him all that well, Linda says. It was pitch black and they were flashing lights in our faces and I don't think you could say it was him for sure.

Maybe you're right, Chaz says. But it shook me. It was my good buddy who told me this guy offed himself some time back.

Linda dabs at Chaz's forehead. Hush now. You know how men are when they lose their women. Sometimes they go to pieces and never get it all back together. It's a shame, it really is. That's why we're so lucky we got each other at a time of trial like this.

Chaz takes out his wallet and lays it on the table. These are our two, Brittany and Jack. He pushes the wallet across the table and Stace looks down at the snapshots: cloudy blue backgrounds, school portraits. The children are ten years old or so, the girl with braces and gold glasses, the boy cowlicked hair and narrow smiling face.

They were asleep in the back. We were on our way back from a meeting and we had to stop and pick up a side of beef from her sister's freezer. Linda's sister's husband butchers us a cow every year. That's why we were on the road so late.

We got to talking, Linda says. I don't see my sister very often.

People who're sleeping don't get hurt so bad in an accident because they don't freeze up, Chaz says. It's like a drunk. They're relaxed so they don't get hurt.

I'm sure they're alright, Stace says.

They're good kids, Linda says sadly, closing the wallet.

Chaz covers Linda's hand with his. We pray they're safe, he says, wherever they are.

Amen, says Linda. I'm trying to be strong, she says.

I know that, Chaz says, looking hard across the table at Stace as he squeezes her hand. I know that.

Stace turns away, surveys the room, catching the eye of a thin, moustached man curled up in an armchair. The man drops the magazine he has been pretending to read and he unfolds himself from the chair, ambles over to the red rope barrier.

Coffee, tea, morphine, Demerol, anything I can get for you folks tonight?

He is wearing a shawl neck cardigan and tartan slippers, the foam soles worn through and flapping as he walks.

Just kidding.

He steps over the rope. Mind if I have a seat? he asks, pulling up a chair and propping knobby elbows on the table top.

What's up with her? he asks Chaz, without taking his eyes off Linda, who is crying into a scrap of tissue. Domestic troubles?

Stace feels anger rising, and he reaches for the man's arm, takes hold of his elbow.

Easy now, tough guy, the man says, looking at Stace, as if noticing for the first time that Stace is at the table.

Leave them alone, Stace says, putting pressure into his grip.

Oh, the man says, raising an eyebrow, appraising Stace. He offers a hand, as quickly retracts it, shows his teeth in a feral smile. New here, are you? All of you? Just in tonight? How wonderful. Any of you play bridge?

Stace and Chaz look at each other. Stace releases the man's arm. Chaz's knuckles are white, all the blood gone from his fingernails where he is gripping the edge of the table.

The man catches their glance, slaps his hands on the table. My name is Chester, he says. I've been here about six years. Welcome to the lodge. He strokes his moustache, watching their reactions.

Six years? Chaz turns to the man, and Linda dabs at the corners of her eyes, turning also to look at the man.

That's right, friends. Chester. The man holds a skinny hand out again and when Chaz reaches automatically for his hand, Chester whips the hand away as if on fire and laughs silent and gape-mouthed in Linda's face.

Stace grabs Chester's arm again and drags him half out of his chair. What the fuck are you talking about, six years?

Chester slides off his chair and around the corner of the table onto Stace's bench. Stace releases his arm and pushes Chester away.

Chester reaches across the table and grabs Chaz's wallet, opens it to the snapshots of the two children. Nada pasquada. I haven't seen them come in, he says, tapping the photographs. They're not here.

They're not here? Linda asks. Her hand trembles beneath Chaz's hand.

Not here, Chester repeats. And that's a good thing, my friends. Take a look around. Would you want your precious ones to be in here with this unhappy lot of sad sacks?

The three look around the room.

I thought not. Chester drums his fingers on the table.

What the fuck is this place? Stace asks. It's like a goddamn old folks home.

Let me show you something. Chester gets to his feet and looks down at the three of them in the booth. Come on, he says to Stace.

Stace nods at Chaz and Linda. I sure hope you find your kids, he says.

Chester scissors his legs over the barrier. You coming? he asks Stace.

Stace slides out of the booth and steps over the rope.

It was an old hunting lodge, Chester says over his shoulder, leading Stace between the tables. About sixty years ago it burned to the ground. You can see the scars of the fire on some of the big trees around the building. The owners were German, and they couldn't afford to rebuild after the war. They lost everything. The story is they were ruined financially and killed themselves, a murder-suicide pact. He slit her throat and then hanged himself over her body.

Cheery, Stace says.

Chester stops at one of the tables, takes an empty bottle from a pocket of his sweater. He touches an older woman on the shoulder. Helga, he says loudly, into her ear.

The woman twists around in her lounge chair, surprised. She has been doing needlepoint in her lap, a design in brown and red that looks like a plate of spaghetti and meatballs.

Schnapps, Chester says, holding the bottle out in front of the woman.

The woman reaches nearsightedly for the bottle and Chester draws it away. Later, he says, patting Helga's meaty shoulder. In a few minutes.

The woman nods slowly, her hand drooping back to her lap.

It gets her every time, Chester says to Stace. She hasn't had schnapps in decades and she still remembers.

He scans the room. Helmut is around somewhere, he says. I hope you meet him. He carries a pipe sticking out of his mouth. You can't miss him. He's wearing lederhosen and clogs. Wooden clogs. There's a photo of them above the fireplace. Happier days.

They stop together at a row of cribs lining the far wall of the room. Chester pulls a pink quilt back. A baby with a dented head frowns up at Stace, it's chubby face skeptical, purple.

We call this one Billy, Chester says, tucking the quilt. He moves to the next crib. Josie. She never made it to her first birthday. She's been here almost as long as I have. I don't think she's ever leaving.

What about you?

I have hope, Chester says, peering into the next crib. One day someone will find me and I'll get out of here.

What's that supposed to mean? What's your story?

Chester smiles down at the crib. Here comes Emmett, he says. He's going to take you for your interview.

Stace watches the silver-haired man wend his way through the tables and clusters of chairs.

Emmett stops at Stace's elbow, looks down at the infant in the crib.

I see you've met Chester, he says to Stace.

Hello, Emmett, Chester says.

We need to ask you a few questions, Stace, Emmett says. I want you to come with me.

Chester whistles. That was fast, he says. That other couple have been here hours. Are you fast-tracking this one?

Let's go, Emmett says to Stace, laying a hand on Stace's shoulder.

Just a second, Stace says, shrugging off the hand. What the fuck is going on? What's this interrogation bullshit?

Emmett cuts his eyes at Chester. We have to ask you a few questions, to clarify some details for us. A bit of necessary paperwork. I'm sure you have some questions of your own. We're going to do our best to answer them, and get you out of here as quickly as possible, if we can.

Fuck it, Stace says. I got no questions, and I don't want to answer any, either. I could give a shit what you all do here.

He's a hard one, Chester says to Emmett. Watch him.

Emmett takes a lighter out of his pocket and flicks the sparker with a black thumbnail. Get out of my sight, Chester, he says quietly.

I'm one of the lucky ones, Chester says to Stace, backing away. We'll see where you fit in, won't we?

Emmett holds Stace with his eyes. I'll tell you this only once, he says, so listen carefully. Everything that happens to you from now on depends on your answers. No bullshit, just the facts.

Emmett cups a hand over the flame, holds the flame close to his skin. I don't know who you are, where you've come from, or how tough you think you are. All that means nothing to me. All that gets boiled away here. What we're left with, what we get down to, is the core. The part of you you haven't ever taken time to look at. Know what I'm saying? The essence. Some people come in here and they're close to that already. They've lived an examined life. Whatever made them tick, they know what it is. But not you. You haven't done that. My job is to help you ask those questions. Because you have to get there. You will get there.

He releases the lighter and holds the palm of his hand up for Stace to see.

Nothing. There is no mark from the flame.

Stace looks past Emmett to the black and white photograph askew above the fireplace mantel. The man in lederhosen and bulky sweater, a pair of skis casually cradled in one arm, his other arm around a young Helga, outfitted in white. The two of them leaning together on the clean-swept, wide wooden steps of the lodge. Happier days.

You must burn away everything you think you know.

He looks at the photograph and thinks of his father. He was once this age. What did he know then, at this age?

The room blurs and he knuckles his eyes and clears his vision and Emmett is still looking at him.

It's not a matter of choice, Emmett says. Do you understand? That's a luxury you no longer have.

Alright, Stace says, tired. Fuck it. Do what you gotta do and get this over with.

Emmett holds his hand, palm up, toward the door.

RED TRUCK

IT WAS NOT SO EASY as all that. Between them they had got Stace into the red truck and the blanket tucked snug around the shoulders and a ball cap pulled low over the sunken face so it could have looked like he was sleeping upright in the passenger seat of the truck. Both Wes and Tanya are sweating though the temperature has dropped further and they can see their breath fogging red in the light of the Exit sign.

Wes is wearing translucent latex gloves he purchased earlier at a service station. He climbs into the cab of the truck and rolls the window down a crack. Follow me, he says to Tanya.

He turns the key in the ignition and the engine turns over but doesn't catch.

He tries it again and they can both hear something switch over but nothing happens. The truck will not start.

I don't fucking believe it. Wes opens his door and jumps down and opens the hood of the truck. Get me a flashlight, he says. Wind tugs the words from his mouth. He peers into the dark cavity.

For awhile Wes stands with both hands on the top of the radiator, looking at the engine, thinking to himself, then he gets back in the truck and tries the starter again. Nothing. Tanya switches off the flashlight and looks up into the night sky. Above the roofline of the motor inn the moon is suffusing snow clouds with a faint glow.

We can't take him back to the room, Wes says. It's crazy. Someone's bound to see us. And we can't leave him in the truck.

It's almost five, Tanya says, pressing the button on her illuminated watch.

Far across the parking lot a man is climbing down from one of the Kenworth sleepers, coffee thermos in hand. He heads across the road to the service station. A light goes on behind drapes in one of the motor inn windows above them.

Let's make this quick, Wes says.

They lower the tailgate and get Stace out from the front and together carry him around the back of the truck and up into the truck box. The baseball cap is knocked off and skids across the pavement. They climb into the back of the truck and, squatting one on either side, wrestle the body until they have jammed it widthways across the box above the wheel wells. They cover the body with the blanket. From a toolbox behind the seat they get a tarp and bungie cords. Wes wraps the tarp over the body, securing it to the sides of the truck box with cords.

He puts the truck in neutral and together they push it across the parking lot until it runs up against the curb by the entrance.

They watch the trucker climb back up into the Kenworth and start the tractor up. Twin plumes of diesel in the pre-dawn air.

I need some tools, Wes says. I'll fix whatever's wrong as soon as I can, but we can't take a chance and run it into the bush before night now. Looks like we're here for the day, anyway. We gotta stay away from the truck.

The blue tarp pops in the wind.

Just hope that stays put, he says.

INTERROGATION

HEY BABY, you're new here.

They are walking down a long dim hallway lined on both sides by doors and the girl hangs out of one of the doorways, her eyes ringed with dark circles and a jagged cut on her throat like a slipped smile.

I hope you're not like all these other deadbeats. She is wearing a dirty pink halter top that is grey in the half-light and tights with stirrups, and even in the available light Stace can see her face is blanched, bloodless, her lips almost white.

They walk past the girl and Stace glances in. Floor to ceiling bunks are stacked, three high, each narrow bed with a humped shape under a blanket. There are a dozen bunks in the room: one, the girl's, Stace supposes, with the blanket in a heap at the foot of the bed.

The girl follows them with her eyes, blows a silent kiss.

I'll always be here for you, she calls out.

In each room they pass, grey bunks, stacked to the ceiling with sleeping people.

In the corridor, cots have been arranged head to toe outside the rooms, between the doorways, each cot with a sleeping person. An old woman, her eyeglasses folded on the bedclothes beside her, slippers on the floor beneath her cot. A young man with tattooed arms folded over his chest, a dull gold crucifix laid against his lips, his eyes open unblinking to the ceiling as they pass. An old man in coveralls on a stepladder is in the hallway unscrewing the light bulbs. As he stretches up, soft rotten gas eases out of him.

The five kids come toward them, led by a middle-aged woman. Three boys, two girls. The kids scuff their feet as they shuffle along. Check this out, one of the boys laughs. He jumps up and slaps his hand against a fire bell. The bell rings flat and metallic. Check it out. The boy's laughter echoes in the corridor.

Stace follows Emmett down the dim aisle between the cots.

They stop at a closed door at the end of the hallway and Emmett raps on the door with one knuckle.

Come in, a muffled voice commands.

After you, Emmett says, opening the door for Stace.

Stace steps into the room and sees a woman sitting at a desk. Behind her, a large window throws back the reflection of the woman's chair and the blue rectangle of a computer monitor, the rest darkness, though the sky is a lighter shade of night above the tops of the trees.

Sit down, she says, without looking up from the computer screen. In the blue glow he sees she is young, maybe his own age, a pale serious face with short dark hair falling around her jawline in a bob. Bracelets on her forearms jangle as she taps at the keyboard.

Before the desk a single chair on a strip of frayed carpet.

His own standing shape black and featureless in the window. He does not recognise himself, now. A dizzy or floating feeling, as if he is in two places at once, separated from himself by the width of a hand. A half-second lag between thought and movement.

Behind him, Emmett unfolds a metal chair and sets it up for himself in the hallway, closing the door so Stace and the woman are alone in the office.

How are you feeling? she asks, stopping typing.

Stace lowers himself into the orange vinyl chair, rests his hands on the smooth wooden arms.

She reaches up and pulls a chain and switches on a brass desk lamp and looks at him for the first time. There is an engraved plastic nameplate on the desk in front of him: Miki. She must be Japanese, he sees now.

I'm sorry, he says at last, though he had no intention of saying that when he thought to speak.

You're sorry, the woman repeats. She picks up a pen and slides a pad of notepaper towards herself. Alright, we'll start there, she says. Why? Why are you sorry?

He looks around the cramped office. Tan cardboard boxes are stacked tidily on metal shelves, the boxes labelled by hand in chronological order, top left to bottom right, a solid wall of boxes.

I don't know, he says. I didn't mean to say that.

That sounds like a favourite answer of yours, she says. 'I don't know.' What do you know? Why do you suppose you're here?

He says nothing, watching her reflected in the window, his own shape there too, black and still.

This is an important question to answer, she says softly. You must answer. She puts down the pen and folds her hands. On the desk beside her a small sheaf of polaroid photographs, his face at the top of the pile, slack and apparently sleeping. It must have been taken in the motor inn while he was lying paralyzed on the bathroom floor.

We're not the police, she says. All that is gone. She waves her hand dismissively. That whole life—gone. So there is nothing left but us here, and the truth will be told.

Her eyes are on his face, searching.

Do you understand what I'm saying?

He looks at her and he is standing in a tunnel of leaves, looking down at the man on the ground. He has spread the plastic wide on the grass and the man's ruined face is looking up into the poplar trees.

Yes, he says to her. I understand what it is you're talking about.

She glances at the computer screen and then back at him. You're twenty-nine years old. We're going to take a little time and you're going to give me an answer—what it is that you're feeling. Surely that's not too much to expect?

He searches for something plausible. I'm feeling tired, he says. And angry.

Angry? She writes it down on the pad.

He begins to feel annoyed. What do you mean by that—'Angry?' I know what I'm feeling. Tired. And angry.

But there's more to it than that, isn't there, she says. Of course you're tired and angry. That goes without saying.

He leans forward in the chair and resists the urge to sweep his arm across the desk and bring it all crashing to the floor. Emmett waiting outside the door like a guard. He touches her plastic nameplate instead, squaring it to the edge of the desk.

So what is it you want me to say?

She picks up the pen. What happened tonight? Tell me about that. We can work back from there if need be.

As clearly as he can he tells her what he did this night, leaving out nothing that he can remember. She writes as he speaks, pen poised above paper when he pauses, his eyes focused over her bent head, looking at his own silhouette in the black window. It is easy to talk now, in fact it is a relief to tell her what she wants to hear. And why shouldn't he? He feels strangely free as he talks. Like some poison is sweating its way out of his system. Something peeling away from his heart.

She slides a photograph out from the pile and turns it toward him on the notepad. Tell me about this, she says.

He looks at the photograph and Dickey's face is staring up at him in black and white. He is lying on his back in the dirt of the driveway where he fell, the front of his T-shirt soaked through grey. A blur of something white obscuring one corner of the photograph—a piece of cotton fluff caught mid-air in the moment of the camera's shutter.

The woman slides another photograph out from the stack, lays it alongside the first. And this? she asks.

Dickey's face clouded, swathed in plastic wrap, eyes closed this time. With one thumb Stace could blot out the entire face.

Yes, Stace says. I did that. It was me. His mouth is so dry he cannot continue.

A bubble of blood had collapsed and turned into a thread that ran down from one corner of Dickey's mouth, across his jaw and had collected in a dark bead on the lobe of his ear. A fly was buzzing around Dickey's head and Stace swatted it away and the fly came back and landed on the open eye. Stace had laid the roll of plastic down and cut a section he thought long enough and he spread the plastic open on the dirt. It was best to do this quickly, he decided. He took Dickey by the shoulders and he seemed to shrink into himself somewhat and Stace saw the front of Dickey's shorts were soaked through with wet and he smelled urine at the same time he noticed the grey stain. It may have been fear but more likely it had been an involuntary action and Dickey had had no control over that last betrayal of his body. Blood was pooling on the sheet beneath the body and he slid Dickey to the centre of the smeared plastic. He had finished with the knife and he dropped it between the man's thighs and picked up a garden trowel. With the trowel he scraped away the dark wet dirt beneath where Dickey had first fallen, where some of his blood had soaked into the ground, and he transferred the small scoopfuls of dirt and gravel and tough shoots of quack grass to the plastic. And when every bit of that ground had been scraped clean he scuffed it all over with his boots and it was as if the only thing left as a reminder was the long sheet of plastic and Dickey lying there in the yard with his arms at his sides.

He laid the trowel down next to Dickey and stripped off the bloodied garden gloves and dropped them to the man's chest. He drew on a clean pair of green rubber gloves and squatted down and carefully folded in the edges of the plastic, staying away from the blood, until the whole thing was tightly wrapped and ready for taping. His hands were slick with sweat inside the rubber gloves. It was impossible to get the duct tape started off the roll without using his fingers, so he pulled off one of the gloves and slid his nail under the leading edge of the tape and eased it back so that he could grip it firmly with his gloved fingers. It didn't seem like he would have left any fingerprints on the roll of tape, but he would dispose of that too, now.

Stace dried his hand against his pant leg and put the glove back on and thought about what he was going to do with the body for the rest of the day, until nighttime. And there was the kid to think of as well. He had not planned on the kid.

He walked over to the Jeep and saw a paper bag of groceries on the back seat. Almost hidden beneath the passenger seat was the yellow rubber tit of a baby bottle. He reached in and picked up the white plastic bottle and brushed off the bits of grit and dog hair that stuck to it and he saw it was mostly full of warm milk. He opened the baby's hands and tucked the bottle into its grasp and guided the bottle to its mouth. The kid started sucking, its eyes on him.

He didn't know how to talk to the baby so he said nothing. He'd always thought he liked kids but it was getting harder to relate to them all the time. Lillis Rae certainly had no time for kids in her life.

The sun was coming around the garage roof and starting to bear down on the open Jeep and he knew it would be very hot soon.

He checked the fingertips of the gloves. They were clean.

He walked around and opened the passenger door and unbuckled the carrier seat and lifted it out by the top handle and carried the kid in it to the shade around the side of the garage. How's that bottle? he asked the kid.

Dickey had a little shed with canvas walls where he had piled wood for the winter. A shaky pile of oil filters on a greasy circle of gravel, the broken handle of a rake in the grass. A stiff pair of work gloves lay on the stump Dickey had used for splitting wood, and Stace pulled the gloves on over the rubber gloves to save the rubber gloves from tearing. He moved half the wood aside, stacking it neatly and quickly on the scruffy ground; when he had cleared a space large enough, he carried the man as best he could over to the shed and laid him in the gap between the two banks of wood. It would certainly do for the rest of the day, if anyone came by the house looking for Dickey. Stace pulled the canvas over the wood pile and weighted it as before with dry branches and put the work gloves back and all the time the kid was sucking at the bottle. He seemed to be enjoying himself in the shade of the garage, kicking his bare feet in the weeds, resting quiet in the plastic carrier seat.

He pushed the garage door up and put the Jeep inside and cleaned the rifle and laid it in the rack and closed the garage. The keys to the Jeep he hid inside the drain spout at the corner of the garage and then he went and picked up the kid in the seat.

His car was down the hill, hidden from sight of the road behind a berm of earth that had been pushed up for some reason years ago. He wasn't sure what exactly he was going to do next, but before he reached the car he would figure it out. Maybe he was in shock, he thought, running on adrenaline, but he felt fine and clear-headed and he had a hard-on, which surprised him. It felt good, crammed against his leg down the front of his jeans. He smiled and then he remembered what he was carrying and he looked down at the top of the kid's head and walked the rest of the way to the car in silence. The June sun beat down through the trees and the sound of locusts zinged through the afternoon like a continuous electric field surrounding him and the baby.

Yes, he says to the woman, I did that.

Something has gone wrong, vastly wrong, and maybe she is not judging him but nevertheless something is hanging over the room and she is waiting for him to talk though it seems like she knows exactly what it is he has done and is simply waiting for him to say it aloud so it can be entered in the notepad in her handwriting.

Through the window the sky is lightening and a big white disc takes shape against the trees and he sees it is a satellite dish catching some of the light and glowing faintly in the nearing dawn.

He knows how it ends, but not how to get there.

I guess I've been on a losing streak for some time, he says. I haven't done some of the things I set out to do and some of the things I never thought I'd see myself do have come easy.

Under the brassy yellow light the woman, Miki, is watching him, and for an instant her face drifts into two out-of-focus planes and he can see behind her face the hollow sockets of her skull, a death's head shining through skin, and he blinks and the vision is gone and she is waiting for him to continue, pen resting on the page.

Why did you kill yourself? she asks.

Kill myself, he says. No, it wasn't like that.

You were drinking. And there were the drugs. A bad combination. You knew better than that.

I guess I wasn't thinking, he admits.

That seems to be fairly common in your life, she says. Would you say you're a smart man?

I knew better than to mix the drugs and the alcohol, yes, he says. But I liked the feeling. You'd have to do it to know what I'm talking about. I could feel my heart beating all the way down in my stomach.

So you did kill yourself.

He shakes his head. It was an accident, I know it.

What were your thoughts?

He can only summon up Tanya's naked back and the darker hair at the nape of her neck.

My ex-wife, he says. Lillis Rae. I was on my way to see her.

And there was a postcard, Miki says. Tell me about the postcard you wrote.

We were never actually married, Stace says. I call her my ex-wife because I wanted to separate her from what I had done that day and I didn't know how it would all turn out. If I had been caught and done time I didn't want her ties to be with me so I wanted to cut myself loose from her. Leave her free to make her own decisions for a life that didn't revolve around me. The postcard was an explanation of what I had done that June day.

A confession?

He thinks about the word, and it seems to fit. Alright, he says. A confession.

Like a suicide note, Miki suggests.

He shifts in the chair. I think maybe I wrote it down to get it fixed in my mind, what I had done, and then I would say it to her anyway and not bother mailing the card. So no, not a suicide note, because I had no thoughts of killing myself. I figured it would be easier to put it on paper than to say it to her.

Miki seems satisfied by this and writes for a bit and then she puts pen and paper aside and leans back in her chair.

He sees the underside of her arms are mottled with faint brown marks, perhaps burn tissue, and twin scars, thin as cuts, that have been hidden by the bracelets on each wrist.

What is it we're doing here? he asks. I'd like to know what it is you're getting at. This whole place. These clothes. What's with this? Stace plucks at the white coveralls.

Look at the back of your pants, Miki says. Look at the cuffs.

The back of the white coveralls are spattered with mud thrown up by the soles of his hiking boots.

That's why, Miki says. We have to keep your original clothes as clean as possible. Same with your boots. We don't want any stray dirt or confusing evidence when it's all over for you. We have strict protocols around the transfer.

She looks at him appraisingly and then turns her head toward the wall of filing boxes.

We collect information, she says. Our main task is to document everyone that comes under our jurisdiction. Photographs by our people, my written report, your comments: everything goes in those boxes. Cause of death, whether it is suicide or not, is the most important criteria for us. Sometimes it's clear, sometimes not.

So this is it, Stace thinks. He closes his eyes hard, opens them. His eyes are burning. Nothing of this is how he expected it to be, though what he did expect he is not sure. He expected nothing. He realises he has never thought beyond the moment. As if for his entire life he has always been looking straight down at the ground beneath his feet. Here. Here. Here. Never ahead. Rarely backward into the past.

It's a relief to know where he is. Though relief is not what he wants to feel. He has started out on some difficult journey and there is a weight to that knowledge, a burden he feels it is right that he bear.

Miki leans forward and rests her arms on the desk. If it's suicide, you become one of us, she says. An attendant. You work here. This whole institution is for processing the dead. I'm a suicide. She holds up her wrists in explanation. Emmett is a suicide. The other workers—all the staff here are suicides. We're here to help the dead get to where it is they have to go.

I met a guy, Chester, out there, Stace says. Why's he here?

All the dead here are waiting for their death to be discovered by the one who matters most to them. Chester died about six years ago, murdered by a hitchhiker. His body has never been found, and he'll be here until it is, which may be never. Some of the dead have no one: we've got some that go back more than a century. The oldest on record is a cartographer who travelled with an early mapping expedition from back east. Our archives aren't complete, but it seems they fade away, get transferred, after about a hundred fifty years, whether they're found or not. We don't know why. The couple you met tonight, Chaz and Linda, will be found later this morning sometime, when a highway maintenance crew sees the broken guard rail. They'll be transferred out of here in a few hours.

What about the guy I shot? Stace asks. What about Dickey?

He's waiting for you, Miki says. You'll meet him later today.

Miki is talking but he is thinking now about Lillis Rae. It is afternoon and they are still at the table. On a plate, the crust from a sandwich she made was drying. The air thickening and darkening between them. Cups, saucers, hands, becoming blurred and forgotten in the dusk. Nothing moved in the kitchen, only Lillis Rae's voice. Outside the house, the cicadas.

Where is it you want to go?

He had made up his mind. Behind, everything was erased. Ahead, he could see only her hand on his arm, which would not last more than a few minutes now. He had no part of the past, no part of a future. His head rushing like a clock, counting backward to some invisible room in the middle of his chest, the zero of silence. How he had got there he did not know, the length of the trail spooling out crazily the length of a whole poisoned life.

She said, You look tired, as if you have not slept in a year. He nodded. Doors were opening everywhere and there was an electric hum in the house. She had turned on the television though he had not seen her leave the room.

He counted to ten. When he reached ten, he knew there was no option but to continue.

You'll never come back. Her words printed in the air so clearly that he could see them floating in a ribbon above the kitchen table.

At the table he had made up his mind. The duffel bag bucking against his knee as he carried everything with him, away from the house.

Right now, I'm not sure if I love you or hate you, she had said.

I'll explain it to you, he said, but it was obvious, even to him, that he was lying.

I'll try to forget about you, she said. Our life. Now I see what it all meant to you. At least now my eyes have been opened.

His own arms heavy on the armrests of the chair, the wood stained dark from hands like his. How many hands? The chair looked to be from the 1970s. He had seen similar chairs in the lobby of a hospital, once. How many had sat in this very chair, in front of this desk? Hundreds? Thousands?

The sky paling, colour seeping back into the world. Out the window, a man, barely visible, climbs a ladder up the back of the satellite dish. The man carries a flashlight, the beam angling up into dark trees that have not yet found green.

This I will try to remember, he thinks. The room, the chair, my hands. I will try to hold onto this, if nothing else.

Where you are going, we have no idea, Miki says. It's already started for you, the process. Just a minute ago, you saw something in me, saw death in my face. I could feel that happen in you.

He reaches across the desk and takes the polaroid of the dead man. The eyes are paler than the face. Dickey must have had blue eyes.

Does this surprise you? Miki is asking him.

He sets the photograph back on the desk.

I mean, we do not know where it is the dead go when they leave here. What becomes of them after the transfer. You pass through here and all we have left are these photographs, these reports. Miki tucks the polaroid into the folder on her desk. We guide you as far as we can, but there is a point at which we can help no further.

I'm trying to understand, Stace says.

We're not like you, Miki says.

I have to see her one last time, he says. It's what I came to do.

Good, Miki says. Then you understand. She looks at him. Stace can't tell how old she is: there is something in her he can't read. As if she is very tired and continues on through force of will.

She says, Emmett will take you there.

And Dickey?

He'll tell you himself what it is he needs.

Perhaps the postcard?

That may be a place to start, Miki says.

The door opens and Emmett sticks his head into the office.

Stace's ready now, Miki says. She looks up at Emmett and then nudges a metal wastecan forward with her foot. Emmett steps around the corner of her desk and drops something feathered and bony into the trash. He licks his thumb and glances at Stace.

Ready to go? he asks.

There is a drop of fresh blood on Emmett's chin.

Go ahead, Miki says to Stace. You know what it is you need to do. She looks tired, drained.

I need your boots, Emmett says. I got a pair for you to trade.

Stace pulls his boots off and hands them to Emmett, who tucks the boots into the nylon bag. The pair of hiking boots Emmett offers are a half size too big, the cleated soles muddy, the suede uppers stiff with dirt.

Put them on, Emmett says. They're close enough to your size.

Miki inks a stamp on a purple pad and stamps a piece of paper and initials next to the stamp and hands the paper and a sheaf of documents to Emmett. Your map's in there, and instructions. Pick up a compass from the supply room.

Emmett puts on his glasses and flips through the papers.

Dickey? he says. I haven't seen him here for months.

He's been out in the bush, Miki says. There's an abandoned trailer somewhere near the reservoir. It's marked on your map. Dickey's been staying out there. Waiting.

He's expecting us for the transfer? He knows I'm coming in with Stace?

Miki nods. We got in touch with him a few hours ago. He knows to meet you there later this morning. I'm sure he'll be there.

Nice weather for bushwhacking, Emmett says. He closes the sheaf of papers and looks at Stace.

Lace up your boots, he says. They look too big for you.

When he looks back through the closing door, Miki is blue over the keyboard, the lamp switched off, her hands motionless in the glow of the screen.

Stace has no idea how long this night has been.

SATURDAY 3

EMMETT

THE VAN THEY LEAVE above them on the fire road, nosed in under the trees, and they cross down into the slash. In the dark they use the flashlights to pick out the narrow deer trail through chest-high scrub of willow and aspen. The sky above the trees lighter now with snow, the first flurries invisible until, like ash, the snow drifts into the tangled cones of their lights. Stace puts up the hood of the coveralls and sleet scratches at the back of his head. He can feel the cold, the wind blowing right through the cotton, but it doesn't bother him. Perhaps he has forgotten what cold means. A word floating in his brain, cut off from definition.

Below, at the far edge of the slash, Emmett stops for him, breath steaming in the light as he pushes aside the low, sweeping boughs of a balsam fir, squats with the nylon bag. A scattering of deer droppings in a hand-size cluster of pellets, fresh black on the needle-strewn earth beneath the tree.

Emmett pulls a glove off with his teeth and sets his flashlight on the ground. He unzips the nylon bag and pulls a rumpled map from an inside pocket, a compass.

Give me some light, he says, spreading the map over his knees. He slips a pair of wire-rim glasses onto his nose and the lenses immediately fog over.

I can't see a damn thing with these glasses, Emmett says. You'll have to read the map.

Stace leans in behind him, holding his flashlight over Emmett's shoulder, tracing with a finger the route ahead, the compass pouched in a crease of the map.

We're near, Emmett says. You recognise the lay of the land?

Stace nods. Sure, he says. I never come at it this side before, that's all. It's a back way I never used.

Five minutes, not more, Emmett says. You need to rest, but we're near. I want to get there by dawn.

Emmett folds the map away, pockets the compass. From the parka he takes a small silver phone and he punches in a string of numbers and presses Send and holds the phone to his cheek.

Emmett, he says into the phone. We'll be there soon.

When Stace opens his mouth a fist of cold air slides into his throat. The must of decay, fallen leaves going back to earth in lank grass. Bracken ferns bleached by frost, the rusted leaves of a waxberry bush, white berries bobbing like lost coins in the gloom. He looks up through the boughs of the fir. It is almost light, the dark evaporating.

How you feeling? Emmett asks, tucking the phone into a pocket.

Fucked up, Stace says.

You feel any pain?

Stace shakes his head, No.

Pain is like a beautiful palimpsest, Emmett says. Look for its traces beneath the surface of everything.

A what?

A palimpsest. A mark, like a brand. A very faint mark.

I want to ask you a question, Stace says.

Go ahead.

You don't have to answer.

Alright.

How did you...? Stace trails off, making a short slashing motion across his throat.

Kill myself?

Yeah. Kill yourself.

Emmett takes a knife and opens the blade and puts the point of the knife under a fingernail and scrapes out a small black shaving that he blows off the blade.

You asking because you want to know, or you asking because you don't know what else to talk about?

I guess I want to know, Stace says.

I drank myself to death, Emmett says after a moment. Simple as that. Crawled inside a bottle and decided not to come back out.

That's not killing yourself.

It took some time.

How did they prove that? The lawyers at the lodge—how did they prove it was killing yourself?

Wasn't nothing to prove. Once it was completed, I knew what I had done. It was clear to me. You can't hide that from yourself.

Why?

Why what? Why was it clear to me, or why did I drink myself to death?

Why did you kill yourself?

Emmett folds the knife away and looks at Stace. What is it makes a person keep on living? he asks. Let me put that to you.

Stace is silent, shrugs.

Think on it, Emmett says. Your answer is in there. When you know why it is that people *don't* kill themselves, why they keep on, you'll also know how it is they *can* kill themselves.

Beyond the shelter of the fir the snow is coming down faster, needling in on them in gusts of wind. Emmett hunches deeper into the parka and Stace puts his chin down into his collar and his hands in his lap between his thighs and tries to warm them.

I never made a confession, Stace says as if speaking to his own chest.

I don't need to hear it, Emmett says.

I feel like I've stepped out of the world. Into something different. Like from a lighted room onto a dark porch. I don't know how to be here. What it is I'm supposed to do.

You see things now that you can't understand, Emmett says. You couldn't see them from where you were but they've always been out here, like we are now. He looks around them, taking it all in with his gaze. This is the world as it is, he says. One world outside the other, brighter world. Every time you've heard a dog barking for no reason you could see. A deer swiveling its ears in the underbrush. A horse looking out into the darkness. A cat crouching in the grass. Birds flying out from a tree or a rooftop. They all see us, passing like shadows.

Stace is silent.

You don't have to believe in any of this, Emmett says. Just look where you are.

I guess I never spent any time thinking about it, Stace says.

My knees are killing me, Emmett says. I can't stay down like this. He picks up the flashlight, stands crouched beneath the shelter of the tree. Let's go on, he says.

What about her? I want to see my wife.

Lillis Rae?

Yes. I need to see her.

You should maybe have thought that through a bit more carefully. Emmett slings the nylon bag over a shoulder and pushes out between the grey fir branches and straightens up, the snow whirling around his head. He holds the compass up to his face and the dial is readable now in the dawn light.

They push through a crimson thicket of willow, holding onto cold twigs as they go down a slight embankment. White river stones, stiff frozen grass. An old creek bed, now an icy tangle of undergrowth and stumps. Sweet alder smoke in the air.

Stone clinks on stone.

Stace looks back and sees a woman crouching in the bushes at the top of the river bank, almost invisible, watching the two of them pass. She is wearing a grey blanket like a cloak, her hair pulled over her shoulder in a long braid. At her bare feet a woven basket full of cedar tips. In one hand she holds a long knife, the other resting lightly on the handle of the basket. By her elbow, two small boys are frozen motionless, only their eyes following Stace. Further back in the bush, a man watches silently, a basket resting on his hip. The faces of all four are covered in large open sores.

Smallpox, Emmett says, stopping to look back. There's a lot of them died in this bush. Spend any time out here and you'll see them around. All this valley used to be theirs.

Stace holds a hand up as a greeting and turns to follow Emmett.

They scramble up the other side of the creek bed, clay and small stones turning under their boots. A rusted spool of barbed wire, yellowed grass stiff with frost.

Four magpies in the naked branches of a poplar.

There's the trailer, Emmett points, stepping aside as Stace comes up behind him.

TRAILER

They come out from the trees into a dank clearing and the Holiday trailer is a humped shape dusted white by the snow. He remembers the trailer. An orange tarpaulin has been stretched over the entire trailer and lashed with rotting string to bumper, hitch, grommets, to the flaking electroplated handle on the door. Black mildew is growing where the tarp has lain over the edges of the trailer roof. In a wood frame two rusted propane cylinders under a dirty canvas cover. Dead leaves and pine needles have collected in the sag between the two cylinders. A once-white five gallon plastic bucket, filled with brackish rainwater, frozen over with a cloudy rind of ice.

Emmett crosses the hummocked ground, drops the bag and uses both hands to crank open the metal shutters at the front of the trailer.

We need some place out of this weather, he says. He breaks away the string, opens the flimsy door.

Stace follows him up the aluminum step into the trailer. It creaks on the cinder blocks, the floor canting beneath them. In the light of the flashes their breath hangs frozen in the air.

Sit down, Emmett says. He points to the bench seat on the far side of the table. He pulls the door closed behind them, sets his flashlight on the scarred arborite.

Emmett opens a narrow cupboard, looks in. There's blankets if you want them, he says, sitting down across the table. He knocks back the hood of his parka, lights a candle, a leaf of flame jumping above the dark root of wick.

The lumpy seat cushion is thin and greening with mildew. Stace tests it with the palm of his hand, then leans back on an elbow, resting his head against the side wall of the trailer. In his pocket, he rolls a white berry between his fingers. He remembers someone, an Indian, once called waxberries the saskatoon berries of the dead.

Through the slats of the louvers, he can see a wall of trees.

From the nylon bag, Emmett removes the thick notebook and opens it on the table. He thumbs a stack of polaroids from between the pages and fans them out.

To refresh your memory, Emmett says, glancing across the table at Stace.

I don't know what it is you want, Stace says.

Emmett shakes a pen and scratches at a corner of a page and then he warms the tip of the pen in his mouth to get the ink flowing.

Dickey is being transferred tonight, Emmett says, testing the pen on the paper again. He puts on his eyeglasses, which immediately fog over, and like a blind man he stares fogbound until the temperature of the glasses adjusts to his heat and the lenses clear. He checks his watch and writes something down on the page.

You don't know what that means but it means good news for Dickey.

I don't give a shit about Dickey, Stace says.

I don't suppose you do.

Emmett writes slowly, stopping to tap the pen against the wrist of his other hand.

I don't suppose you've given a lot of thought to it, he says without looking up.

I thought about it some and there was no point, Stace says. What's done is done and can't be mended.

And yet here you are, Emmett replies.

The phone buzzes. Emmett puts the pen down and opens the phone and looks at Stace.

Yep, he says into the phone.

Stace can hear a faint voice speaking and then Emmett says, Hold on, and he puts the phone on the table and spreads the map open and finds what he is looking for. With the pen he circles something and picks up the phone. I'll be right there. Give me about a half hour, he says, snapping the phone case closed.

There is a quiet knocking beside Stace's head, and when he looks up there is a man's face pressed against the smeared window, looking in at him on the damp bench.

Right on time, Emmett says, and gets up to open the door.

Stace's mouth goes dry.

Dickey steps up into the trailer and there are three of them in a space for two and the floor shifts again beneath their feet.

It's not very stable, Emmett says. It should be propped up. The ground's soft here.

Dickey looks at Emmett. I'm not going to sit, he says, his tongue working stiffly inside the cave of his mouth.

He too is wearing a pair of filthy white coveralls, the top half of the coveralls rolled down and held around his waist by a length of string, his upper torso bare. Water is beaded on waxen, translucent skin. The hole in his chest is no more than a small bloodless pucker.

So, down to business, Emmett says, looking at Stace. I don't think Dickey wants to spend a lot of time here with you, which I'm sure you can appreciate.

He turns the papers around on the table and hands the pen to Dickey. Most of the paperwork is done, he says. Sign where I've marked and that's it.

So I'm going out tonight? Dickey asks, taking the pen between thick fingers and bending over the papers.

Sometime after midnight, Emmett says. You should be down at the head of the reservoir by the turn-off before then, but as near as we can predict, you'll be transferred out before sunrise tomorrow.

So what about him? Dickey asks, signing the papers. Why's he here?

He's getting you out, Emmett says. He wrote a postcard before he died, saying where you could be found.

That was mighty thoughtful of him. Dickey hands the pen to Emmett and turns around, staring at Stace.

Emmett initials the papers and tucks them with the photographs into the notebook, snaps the elastic band around the bundle. He returns the map to the zip bag and runs his hand over his jaw.

I'm out of here, he says. Duty calls.

He gets up from the table and slides past Dickey, puts his hand on the door. Try not to kill each other, he says, and steps down from the trailer.

On the table, the flame leans sideways then rights itself.

Through a gap in the shutters, Stace sees Emmett flip up the hood of his parka as he crosses back over the clearing before he disappears into the underbrush.

My kid, Dickey says. He leans against the aluminum coaming of the countertop, tilting his head back to rest on a broken cabinet door. Stares up at the curved roof. My fucking kid. Tell me about my kid.

Snow rattles on the tarpaulin and against the metal skin of the trailer.

I didn't know you would have the kid with you, Stace says.

Seems like there's a lot of things you didn't fucking know, Dickey says. It wouldn't have made a difference if you had known, would it?

I might have done it different.

Dickey folds his arms over his chest. His shadow flickers and jumps. I thought I hated you but that's gone now it seems, he says. You can only hate so long before it costs you too much.

I regret what I did.

What you think or feel means nothing to me, Dickey says. I know you're sorry and what does that do for me? Not a thing.

I wrote a postcard, Stace says.

So I hear.

I wrote down what I did and where I left you, Stace says.

I guess you want I should thank you for that?

Dickey is looking at him and Stace sees he has in his hands a small figure that looks to be made of twisted grass and roots, a man-shaped thing with tendril arms and legs and a knot for a head. Dickey sets the doll on the counter and the doll lays there pooled in shadow.

I guess I'm saying I forgive you and that doesn't mean what it sounds like. It's got nothing to do with you. You learn that. There's no use in hate and no use in carrying all that with you because you need to deal with things as they are. I know where the hate cells are stored up and it's possible to cut those out and be free of that.

I don't give a shit, Stace says.

No you don't, Dickey says. I can see that.

Dickey looks down at the figure twisted up out of grass and roots and with a finger he pushes it over the lip of the sink and there is a small dry sound on metal when the doll falls inside the basin.

I've been waiting for this day, Dickey says.

He looks around the trailer and down into the dry sink and then turns and goes down out of the trailer and closes the door.

Stace puts his forehead against the window. Cold cuts his face where frame and sill do not meet, a draft fluting on the lip of metal. Across the clearing, Dickey squats, naked to the waist, gathering something dropped in the snow. The emaciated curve of his back, the thin buttocks above his bare heels. A black hole in the centre of his spine.

Stace hammers the window open with the heel of his hand.

It is snowing in the trailer.

He lies back on the bench seat, stares up at the cobwebbed ceiling. A dark hand flexing inside his head.

RESERVOIR

THE FACTS, as they must be imagined, are this. A gloved hand holding the steering wheel. A dark road before dawn. Stace stopped the Jeep and turned the lights off. Jesus christ, he said. Jesusfuckingchrist. He got out of the Jeep and puked in the ditch, leaning for support with one hand on the front fender. His wristwatch clicked against the chrome moulding around the headlight. He spat thickly, trying to clear his mouth. He was crying harshly with almost no sound, the muscles of his throat stiff and cramped. He was a stranger to me, he thought. Everything is breathing, but he is not breathing.

It was nearing dawn when Stace reached the reservoir. A thick fogbank hung over the water and drifted like low cloud over the marshlands, greying out the long curving wall of the dam. Trees on the far shore silhouetted against a paler sky. He rolled the wet window down and wiped the rearview mirror with a gloved hand, backed the Jeep slowly down the ramp until the boat trailer was over its axles in the water. He killed the engine and the headlights and sat for a moment in silence in the dark trees, hands on the steering wheel, smelling the dampness coming in through the window.

Sit tight, he said to the kid.

He got down out of the Jeep. The cement ramp was grooved for traction and still it was slippery underfoot. He released the boat, the cold water pressing around his rubber boots and buckling them against his legs. He pushed the boat free of the trailer and caught up the painter line and pulled the boat aground on the side of the ramp, tied the painter line to a sapling. He stripped back the vinyl cover, folded it over the fender of the trailer. He looked into the boat. He had lashed three cinder blocks to the package with a length of white electrical cable he had found in the garage. Through the plastic, clouded with condensation, Dickey's face was turned up at him, his eyes surprised still, his mouth open like there was one last thing he had meant to say.

Already in the boat were Dickey's tackle box, fishing rod, net and a pair of oars. Two faded life preservers, one small, one large.

He started the Jeep and pulled up out of the water to the gravel area at the side of the turnaround. The kid was playing one-handed with its toes, sucking its other thumb, quiet for the moment. He reached over and felt the kid's bare legs. They were cold.

Who's a little tough guy, hey? he said to the kid. Who's a little toughie?

Behind the seat he found a bunched-up towel. He wrapped the towel around the kid's legs and tucked it in at the sides of the carrier seat. The kid reached out and touched Stace's cheek, delicately.

He locked the Jeep and walked down the ramp, carrying a pair of tied-together running shoes. The sky was lightening to the east, the edges of clouds picking up colour, the still water a perfect mirror. Overhead a ragged S of crows flew silent, followed by a lone, cawing crow. Fog drifted slowly away from shore, draining down from the low fields and sedges to rise and thin-out over the water. Small birds twittered from the brush and somewhere from the dark among the reeds he heard a duck call.

He put one foot in the boat and grasped the gunwales, pushing free of the ramp as he stepped forward into the boat, the aluminum hull creaking on the ramp beneath the weight. The boat steadied as he sat on the centre rowing thwart.

He touched Dickey's knees, cold through the plastic, tried to fold the stiff legs out of his way. The knees would not go under the seat.

He guided the oars into the locks and turned the boat until his back was to the centre of the reservoir and he was facing the distant line of the dam. He rowed smoothly and quietly, stopping to unzip his windbreaker when the boat launch and the shore were no longer visible. The tops of the trees were grey behind the mist. He shipped the oars, resting the blades on the stern seat. The boat rocked gently in the centre of the lake. He stripped off the windbreaker and kicked aside his running shoes and knelt in the bottom of the boat. It was light enough now that he could see the plastic was sweating inside with blood.

He got an arm under Dickey's shoulders and pulled the long wrapped bundle up against his body, locking his hands across the chest. He lifted one end of the package over the side of the boat, propped Dickey with one cinder block resting against the transom. Blood ran and pooled inside the plastic. He tried to lift the other end and couldn't get enough leverage. He slid beneath Dickey and half lay in the bottom of the boat with his neck against the rowing bench and used his back to lift. He got the package with the cinder blocks up on the gunwale. The boat tipped sideways until there was only an inch of freeboard above the water. He put a foot on the opposite gunwale and with his other arm pushed straight up so the package lurched up and over and crashed into the water. The boat seesawed, then righted slowly. He got up on the bench and looked over the side. Bright gouges had been scored in the aluminum by the cement blocks. The surface of the water was smoothing already, bubbles still rising, the white sheathing of the electrical cable tinted murky green by algae the last thing he saw before the whole thing faded into the lower dark.

He rowed back toward the boat launch, the oars creaking in the locks, the reservoir silent except for his noise and the calls of ducks in the sedges. When he was near enough to see the ramp through the fog he turned the boat in toward shore and ran in through the lily pads and the pondweed to the reeds, using one of the oars to pole the boat deeper into cover until he ran the hull up against a half-submerged log. He put the oar back into the lock and stripped off his jeans and underwear and rolled them into a bundle and wedged them under an arm, slung the pair of running shoes around his neck. He pulled on the rubber boots again and stepped over the side of the boat, standing precariously on the rotten log, up to his thighs in icy black water, holding steady to the side of the boat. He found his balance and waded the length of the log, steadying himself by grabbing at the hard stalks of tule bulrushes. A wren flicked past his head, punching a hole in his heart, and he stopped and waited until his pulse came back to normal and then he stepped from the log to a tiny muddy clearing under a willow bush. Pondweed clung to his legs. He hung his pants and underwear and shoes over a bush and stood, storklike, on one leg at a time, to empty water from the rubber boots, then used a handful of willow leaves to clean his legs as best he could in the semi-darkness. He pulled on his clothes and the boots and looked back toward the boat. It was invisible amidst the reeds but for the corner of a yellow sticker on the hull.

He pushed under the willow and fought his way up through the rushes, sedges slashing at his legs and branches tearing at the windbreaker. He found a faint trail and followed it through tall wet grasses until he reached the road. His jeans were soaked through, stiff and cold against his legs. He took off the rubber boots and flung one off into a deadfall and the other into a swampy backwater below the road. He laced the runners and jogged back along the road, through the dark woods to the boat launch. High overhead, the tops of the trees were in sunlight now, leaves a virid green canopy, the sky the colour of milk. The road holding murky bowls of sky in its potholes.

The kid was red-faced and crying and the Jeep smelled of shit. He unbuckled the baby seat and carried the kid over to a wet picnic table, set the plastic seat down in the centre of the table. He rested for a moment, hands on his knees, caught his breath.

I bet you're hungry, aren't you little guy?

From the pocket of the windbreaker he took the sandwich he had prepared for himself and opened the plastic wrap and gave the kid the cheese sandwich. The kid dug its fingers into the soft white bread and put the sandwich up to its mouth.

If no one came for hours, the table would be in shade until late afternoon, anyway. He re-tucked the towel around the kid's legs. It would have to sit in its own stink, there was nothing he could do about that. Hopefully the kid could eat the sandwich. With any luck a car would be along within an hour. The ramp was usually busy all weekend, with boat trailers parked along the side of the road practically back to the dam turn-off. It wouldn't take long for whoever showed up to figure out something was wrong: the Jeep and empty trailer parked off the ramp, the kid sitting in the middle of the picnic table, no sign of boat or driver.

He switched the radio on low, to keep the kid company, and then walked to the bottom of the ramp and braced his feet and flung the Jeep's keys far out into the reservoir. The kid looked at the splash and back at him.

Alright, he said to the kid. You're a tough guy, aren't you?

He put his hand on the top of the kid's head for a moment, then bent down and kissed the soft hair. The smell of talcum powder and shit.

Where the road ran beneath the trees it was carpeted in rusty pine needles. In the open, the road was hard and rocky and rutted. Crossways in the gravel on either shoulder of the road, needles and bough tips lay in herringboned, rippled tide marks, left there by spring meltwater flushing down the grade to the ditch. Strung above the road, double swags of power lines, the poles green with preservative, the wood scotched with holes.

When he could run no more he pulled off the windbreaker and tied its sleeves around his waist. He walked for a ways, hands on his hips, sweat rolling down the small of his back and dripping off his nose, his chest on fire. He glanced at his watch then realised he hadn't actually read it and had to bring his wrist up again to look at the watch. He should have been back to the car by now, but it was hard to tell where exactly he was. Ahead, the sound of an engine through the underbrush. He scrambled up an embankment, pulling himself up into the bushes. A station wagon with two men in it roared past, gravel bouncing after the car as it disappeared behind a curve. Dust filtered through the air and settled on the leaves in front of his face. He slid down the bank to the road.

It was a few minutes later that he came to the turnout, the twin ruts almost hidden by new poplar saplings and ryegrass, and he cut off the road and walked up the overgrown track and into the clearing where he had parked his car. The windows of the car pearled and dripping with dew. The abandoned trailer hunched under its dirty orange tarpaulin.

He got into the car and put it in neutral and got it rolling. He steered it back down the track between the walls of trees, saplings and grass bending and scraping beneath the car, until he was almost at the road. He stopped the car and opened his door and listened carefully and except for the clamour of birdsong there was no sound. He started the engine and flicked the windshield wipers to clear the windscreen and pulled out of the track onto the road. It was almost six.

* * *

He turned off the reservoir road and onto the highway and passed no cars. Out in the open the sky was shot through with coral, the green fields stretching out across the prairie in gently undulating swells to the horizon. Past the Old Coach Road he slowed and turned off the highway onto the oiled gravel access road, the car bumping over the railroad tracks at the level crossing. Near the house he swung the car to the shoulder and coasted to a stop. He rolled his window down and put his arm on the door, watching the house. The pole lamp hung above the yard like a faint medallion against the morning sky. In an upstairs window her bedroom light came on. Curtains drawn by a pale arm. For a moment her face in the window, looking up at the sky. Then she turned away from the window.

BACK ROAD

LIGHT SWARMING above the trees.

It has stopped snowing. He is walking down a narrow road. Rotten leaves frozen grey as slate in the ruts.

Somewhere behind him the trailer. Below him, water flashes silver through the brush, the surface of the reservoir flecked and chopped with whitecaps. On either side trees bow and thrash the air. Birds wheel up from the fields beyond the trees, a great fibrillation of wings rippling the sky, blacking out for a moment the low winter sun as the column passes above the road.

How long he has been walking he cannot say. He realises he is carrying the twig doll. He pitches the doll into the ditch and it vanishes among the grasses as if it had been waiting to return to that very spot. He takes a handful of snow from the ditch where it has collected in a giant maple leaf and puts the snow in his mouth.

Trees hold a few golden leaves, like fireworks frozen above him in black branches.

The reservoir curves away and falls back and he is in no country he knows. In the hummocked fields, grass stubble has been trodden by deer in a wavering path which gleams like beaten metal where frost has lain in shadow all day. Forgotten crabapples hang waxen yellow, leaves a rotten mulch beneath black fruit trees. A white farmhouse dark within its windbreak of poplar. A figure appears in an upper window. A girl, shaking a cloth against the side of the house. There is a flickering, shifting quality to the figure, a transparency, as if light were passing through the moving girl.

Stace moves a hand past his face. His eyes shuttering.

The girl leans out the window, her arms flashing, the bright cloth snapping slowly up and down, a semaphore, a movement.

In an open doorway below, figures move in and out of vision, one by one stepping briefly into a rectangle of light and then on into darkness. The house, a head filled with subtle vibrations of light. A man holding a spade flickers in a corner of the farmyard, vanishes as he stoops to brush at his thighs. Four boys race silently across the field, three disappearing simultaneously, the fourth continuing on, his red hair blurred, until he too flickers and vanishes as if stepping through a curtain of air.

Light begins to leak from the sky. A lantern flashes through a window. Dusk. The slow blur of his shadow, his lower legs, as he walks into darkness. More lanterns, windows. Figures in the glow of the lanterns, a girl folding a cloth, a woman pressing her face against the glass, a man holding a child in the frame of a doorway.

He moves his hand past his face, and there is the afterimage of a window, of a woman looking out to the road.

When Stace closes his eyes there is, for a moment, the illusion of forward motion, a vertiginous rush as if his brain had swung in the dark hull of his head.

This is what will stay with him. The rectangle of light, the face printed onto the glass like a collodion negative. The woman is holding a knife or a pen in her left hand.

SUBDIVISION

FAR TO HIS LEFT the lights of her house float in the dark.

Stace steps over a sag of wire, the remains of a fence, and someone has driven a tall iron rod into the ground there, orange plastic surveyor's tape fluttering from the stake. A fresh white three-sided wooden property marker beside it, almost lost in the tall grass.

He kneels on the ground and with the flashlight reads the lettering on the wooden marker. It's the corner of her property, he says, and realises he has spoken aloud.

Around him, where he remembers a field of wheat, the ground has been scraped bare, the clay gouged by tread marks from an earthmover. In the beam of the light he can see the land has been flattened and smoothed over beneath a thin blanket of fresh snow.

He gets to his feet, knocks wet mats of snow off his knees where he has knelt beside the stake. His heels hot and chafing under the rub of the oversize boots.

Even the foundation of the old house is gone, smashed and pulled from the earth. Red bricks, broken underfoot, glint like bloodied teeth in frozen mud. The shelterbelt of caragana that surrounded the old house lot bulldozed into a brush pile with the rubble.

He stands bareheaded in the dark field, the moon overhead barely luminous, a chalky smudge.

He follows the line of surveyor's tape and steps onto a paved road surface. A street sign like a naked tree at the intersection of two deserted streets. One blank arm points south, the other west. The wind-scoured asphalt curves across the prairie with geometric precision, white concrete curbs rising above raw mud flats. He walks down the centre of the road and passes an earthmover and a stack of sewer fittings, the vertebrae of a prehistoric animal. The bucket of a backhoe resting on a length of culvert.

Five new houses without lights huddle together, their backs to him, facing the road, steam whisping silently from chimneys. He cuts across and walks between two of the houses and comes out on a clean, lighted street. A white billboard has been erected at the far end of the crescent, nearest the highway: Show homes open soon.

The houses gape, empty-windowed, blank, above double garages. Fieldstone chimneys made of no stone from around here. A blue dumpster overflowing with wallboard scrap is parked lengthways along the gutter in front of the houses.

Small numbered flags have been planted on the lots facing the row of show homes. The flags make a tearing sound in the wind. Pits for basements have been dug down through the prairie, the holes swimming with shadow.

Out across the dark raw field, past the sodium glow of the street lamps, her house is almost hidden by the long screen of trees which have been left along the fence.

SATURDAY NIGHT 4

FARMHOUSE

He circles in the outer darkness. The farmhouse is as he remembers it. Blue shadows from a television shimmer inside like reflections shaken from water. At the back of the house a glassed-in porch with a narrow window into the kitchen. Through the kitchen window he sees flowered wallpaper, a calendar, a rack of dishes, the top of the refrigerator.

He climbs the three steps and opens the screen door. The porch is cold and his breath plumes in the still, sweet air. The screened cabinet he'd built years ago holds late-harvest apples. On a lower shelf, potatoes, earth-caked and pungent, spill from burlap. She has stacked old newspapers on top of the hutch, the papers bundled with binder twine. On pegs beside the wooden kitchen door her jackets, a broom, a twisted branch of rosemary. A row of boots and shoes beneath.

She is singing. Her voice floats out through the door.

He tries the handle of the wooden door, which is unlocked.

He feels his heart pounding ragged and hard: it seems to have changed rhythm, as if something has shifted inside him, but when he puts his hand on his chest it feels no different than before.

Lillis Rae is sharpening a knife, her back to him, when he steps into the kitchen. Faintly, shouts from the TV at the other end of the house. Sirens. There is the smell of frying meat, vinegar. Lillis Rae puts the knife and stone down on the counter and leans against the stove, pressing her pelvis to hot enamel as she stirs something in a pan on a back burner. There is an illusion of movement as the wallpaper above the stove wavers and warps in heated air. On the counter beside the stove is a bottle of beer. She raises the bottle to the side of her nose, then rubs its cool sweat across her forehead. Her hand obscures the label as she drinks from the bottle. Her throat pulling at the beer. Her eyes open, staring up at the yellow ceiling. Over jeans she is wearing one of his old shirts, a blue one, her hair tied back loosely from her face.

He eases the door closed and stands just inside the kitchen. He sees everything now with a kind of terrible clarity, as if there is too much light in the room. Once he had looked through the viewfinder of a photographer's camera and the room had looked to him more than real, like a composition put together there in the camera, smaller yet sharper, more defined. Perfect in a way a room had never before looked. And so it is now. The kitchen receding yet hard-edged, and he looks around the room, once so familiar as to be almost invisible, trying to see things in the kitchen and fix himself to them, so that he is webbed and held in by these bright things. The humming refrigerator. The dripping tap with the green rag draped over the faucet. The potted ivy trailing down from the bookcase by the table.

He crosses the kitchen behind her and sits in the chair at the end of the table. His old chair.

She lifts a spoon to her mouth, twice. Turning from the stove, she opens a drawer, removes a plastic spice packet, the contents of which end up in the pan. She shakes the pan, lifting it from the heat before taking the pork chop and sliding it onto a plate. From a saucepan she forks a potato, a pair of carrots. She splits the potato with the fork and scrapes drippings from the frying pan onto the open potato.

She sits to eat. A paperback is propped in front of her placemat. She presses the book flat with the palm of her hand and tucks the corners of the book under the edge of her plate.

Stace watches her eat and read and he is close enough to smell her. She does not see him or hear him and he realises there is something he does not yet know. Perhaps it is impossible to reach her, then, he thinks.

He reaches across the table and touches her hand, at rest beside her plate. The skin on the back of her hand warm and finely veined and scrubbed red. I wrap my fingers around her and there is nothing that touches her, he thinks. She cannot feel me.

His own fingers, his arm, heavy and stupid as cement.

Her face is lean and pale, focused down into the book, the face of a woman who has learned to live alone. An attractive face gone tight around the eyes and the mouth, some grey at her temples where he remembers none before. He looks at her and there is a doubling of the light, a drowned face like sorrow surfacing, her face dissolving for a moment and then clumsily recomposing as if to disguise the other hidden beneath.

He is looking at her from across the table and it is more than the table that separates them.

His eyes well up and he feels tears run down his cheeks, run into the corners of his mouth. He rubs them away and laughs at himself. Where has this upwelling come from? There is something artificial feeling about it. He had not known it was there and it feels manufactured for the occasion: too obvious; contrived.

Lillis Rae finishes her meal in silence, rises to clean the plate and cutlery in the sink. Pulls the sleeves of her shirt up by dragging the cuffs with her teeth, exposing the white undersides of her forearms, her hands coming out of the water like mysterious animals. She shakes hair from her face, bends over the sink.

Her movements coded.

She moves and I am still, he thinks. Perhaps nothing ever did belong to him. Not truly. Not to anyone. *The lord giveth and the lord taketh away.* His father had said that to him once. His father had been stewing rhubarb at the stove and he had said that suddenly, from nowhere, and even at that time, at that age, Stace had realised he was talking about his mother though her name was never mentioned. His father had looked out the apartment window as he stirred the rhubarb in the pot and Stace had seen his father's hot, distracted face and had felt embarrassed for his father at that moment. It was as if his father had all that time been carrying on a conversation inside himself and those words had simply come out that afternoon, come out the way an underground spring comes to the surface and then drops below ground again to continue, invisible and unheard. His father had been religious at one point in his life, and there was always a bible on the bookshelf, but the bible was never opened, that Stace remembered. That book had been from some other, earlier life. Maybe that is the secret to life, he thinks now. Earlier selves dissolving slower than any disease, until you look back and recognise almost nothing from the past you have lived. A stranger even to yourself. Your shed selves fragmentary, small, fragile. Even your own history is not truly yours.

And that those words should surface now, from childhood, dredged up by what?

Things of his father's life that only he, Stace, can remember. Things his father, wherever he is at this moment, will have long forgotten. Those words, that afternoon, gone clean from his father's life.

He gets up from the table and moves down the hallway toward the living room, tracing the line of the wainscot with the tips of his fingers. Light filters in through curtained windows at the end of the hall, enough for him to see her framed photographs on the walls. Boiled faces floating under glass. The one photograph of his father missing, a tiny hole where the hook had been fastened in the wallboard.

In the living room the television is on, tuned to a police show. A man with a gun is kicking in a door.

A fancy lamp with a stained glass shade glows on an end table. A bamboo dragon grins up at Stace from the tabletop.

She has rearranged the furniture. Where his albums had been stacked along one wall stands a pressboard rack of CD jewel cases, and a compact disc player has replaced his turntable in the stereo stand. He cannot even remember what music he used to listen to. Another lifetime gone.

The old roll-top desk, which must have been too heavy or cumbersome to move, is still in the same corner, and next to it a folding TV tray with a few straggly plants in mineral-stained clay pots.

Above the desk a framed road map of the country. Phone numbers and addresses have been penned in next to small towns all over the map. The map is full of red holes, where a ballpoint has gone through paper to the cork behind.

Stace seats himself at the open desk. Neatly labelled manila folders with elastic cords separate bills from correspondence. He snaps back the cord on a folder labelled *Correspondence*, removes a handful of letters and postcards. There are postcards from all over the country, most of them addressed from towns marked on the map. Bright photographs of legislative buildings, of grain silos. Truckstops. Lakes with picnic benches. And typescript along the scalloped bottom edges of the cards: *Scenic Green Falls; Capitol City; Winter Sunset; Long Haul Restaurant.*

On the back, brief messages in cramped, grade-school handwriting. Blurred postage marks.

Stace glances at the cards, shuffles them back into the folder. In the bottom drawer of the desk, beneath bundles of bills and stapled sheaves of bank statements, he finds a sealed brown envelope. Thin, fading ink on the front: *Stace*. Inside, the weight of a book. He removes the envelope from the drawer, gently pushes his thumb under the gummed flap. Brittle glue cracks away and he slides the book out into his hand. It's a cloth-bound diary, fastened with a tiny gold lock. He squeezes the hasp between thumb and forefinger, soft metal giving under pressure, and opens the book. Marbleized endpapers. Pages yellowing and brittled by acid.

He flips quickly through the book, stopping at a photograph taped inside the back cover. A black and white snapshot. A young man standing bare-chested beside an old woman seated in a lawn chair, his hand on the back of the woman's chair. Staring down at his naked foot, turned on its ankle in the grass. The old woman's hand coming up toward the camera, as if to wave or to accept a glass of water. Her face sinking under the brim of her hat.

Stace flips the photograph up on its hinge of tape.

A picture of his father, dated on the back. Red pen, a woman's name he cannot decipher, and then beneath that his father's name. He breaks the photograph away from the tape, lays it atop the desk. Flips backward through the diary. A small snapshot slides from the centre of the book: a photograph he remembers was taken in a booth at a bus depot. His own face. A thin dark face tilted up beneath a grey cap. A hard and serious look at the camera in the photo booth, as if in his youth already he had been documenting the moment for posterity.

Stace turns the photograph over in his hands, looks at the date.

He peels sharp, handsome features—teeth, eyes—from the surface of the photograph, pools them white and black in the palm of his hand.

He brings the empty photograph up to his face, presses it to his forehead.

Stace gets up from the desk, taking both photographs, walks down the dark hallway to the bathroom. Closes the door, snaps on the light. He props the photographs against the mirror, leans over the sink to examine carefully his own face before bringing his hands up.

A translucent membrane has started to form over his lower face, sealing over his mouth and nostrils. He touches the membrane lightly with the tips of his fingers. It is pliant and fine as skin, a surface slightly sticky with something like honey. As wide as he can, he unlocks his jaw and opens his mouth, the tissue stretching white over his mouth and then splitting and finally tearing without pain. With a nail he scrapes at the tissue, the new skin rolling back like soft cuticle from his lips, nostrils, coming off against his fingertips. Honey oozing from ducts at the corners of his eyes.

His face beneath the membrane is different from that of the boy's in the photograph. The youthful hardness replaced by something truly hard, something narrow and fierce.

Glancing at the photographs, he moves fingers across his face. He molds bones which shift like wax beneath skin, recomposing his face, pushing his face back into the contours of the face in the photograph.

He lowers his hands.

Looks at the stolen face.

A small skull floating in the back of his brain.

READING LESSON

ABOVE THE NOISE OF THE TV there is the sound of a car coming up the drive to the house. Light splashes across the bathroom wall and ripples through the shower curtain. He puts the photographs down and steps up with one foot on the edge of the tub and looks out the bathroom window into the yard.

It is snowing. Under the flare of the pole light a car parks next to Lillis Rae's muddy International Travelall. The door opens and Tanya gets out of the car, slams her door and walks quickly around the back of the house. She is carrying a plastic grocery bag full of what looks like books. She is here for her reading lesson.

Lillis Rae opens the back door.

It feels like winter, Tanya calls from outside, and then he hears her come up the porch steps and into the house. It's snowing like crazy, Tanya says in the kitchen.

He switches off the light and opens the bathroom door a crack and looks down the hallway to the kitchen. Tanya is taking off her leather coat, propping herself with a hip against the door frame as she heels off running shoes.

You want a beer? I've already had one, Lillis Rae says.

Sorry I'm late, Tanya says, picking up the bag of books from the floor. I had to run home and do some laundry.

You still at the motor inn?

Bob is coming back tomorrow, I think, Tanya says, hanging her coat on the back of a chair. I told him to just pay for the room while he's away. I thought I'd stay there this time instead of all that back and forth. It always seems like I hardly take anything with me and then it's such a pile of stuff to lug back home. It drives me crazy. It's like having two apartments.

Lillis Rae crosses the kitchen to the table with two bottles of beer. You have a chance to do your readings?

Sure. It's going good. Really good.

He hears the caps from the beer bottles fall onto the table and one drops to the floor and spins across the linoleum, rolls toward the stove.

Don't worry about it, Lillis Rae says. I'm not cleaning the floor again before I leave. I'm sick of this fucking floor.

You got a moving date when you're out? Tanya asks.

Nothing final, Lillis Rae says. They showed me the plans. The whole front yard will be asphalt, covered right over. They're going to build a convenience store and a gas bar for the subdivision right here where we're standing.

If I'm around give me a call. You know, packing or whatever. Tanya waves her hand to take in the room. You got lots to move.

I feel like burning it all, Lillis Rae says. All this old shit.

You got some nice stuff here, Tanya says. The roll-top desk, right? But yeah, the fridge and stove are ready for the dump. They got real nice ones in the catalogue now. Nice colours.

I'm going to get a new place, Lillis Rae says. No more creaky, drafty old barns. I guess I liked this place at some point, but not anymore.

Onwards and upwards, Tanya says, raising her beer bottle toward the kitchen ceiling.

Brand new. Clean and white.

It'll be a shame to see your garden go, though, Tanya says. I guess eventually it'll happen all over here. Suburban sprawl. Like cancer.

Onward and upward, Lillis Rae says.

What are they calling the new thing? Quail Run Estates or something? Quail better bloody run, if they know what's good for them. Tanya laughs, bangs her bottle on the table. Quail Run. I don't even remember seeing quail around here. I think those Cooper boys shot 'em all.

Country living for the city folks, Lillis Rae says. Real quails aren't even necessary. Just the thought of them. They always name these places for whatever is gone, what they tear out. Indian names for places Indians can't even go to anymore. And Willow Tree Mall. Remember, there used to be willows all along that creek and when they built the mall they ran the creek underground and paved all the trees under the parking lot. Maybe that's all we're left with. Names for things. Signs that light up. Not the things themselves.

I hope the developers've paid you what the land is worth, Tanya says, taking out a pack of cigarettes. Mind if I smoke?

Lillis Rae gets up and takes an ashtray down from the top of the fridge.

I'm kind of fucked up tonight, Tanya says, lighting a cigarette. She lays the lighter on top of the cigarettes and blows smoke down along the table and looks out the black window.

Bob?

No. Tanya shakes her head. Whatever. The whole situation. Everything and nothing. Same old shit.

You want to try reading a bit? See what kind of progress you've made?

I almost didn't come by tonight. I was going to call and cancel. I'm not sure I feel like doing much. I think I've got a cold or something coming on.

I'm glad you came. You want some tea? I can put the kettle on.

No. Beer is fine. Tanya laughs and blows smoke at the ceiling. I like to burn out a cold. You ever notice how people who don't smoke are always sick?

You need a whiskey to chase that beer.

You got whiskey?

Lillis Rae gets up and pulls her chair over to the stove and gets up on the chair to open the cupboard where they have always kept the liquor.

I've got rye, vodka and tequila. Take your pick.

Oh fuck, Tanya says. No more tequila, please.

She sets the cigarette down on the ashtray and opens her book at the table.

Can you remember where I left off? she asks. It was somewhere around the middle, wasn't it?

Chapter Four, Lillis Rae says, stepping down from the chair. Start there.

Tanya hunches over the book, clears her throat. Using a finger to underline the words, she reads aloud slowly, pausing to drag on the cigarette when she comes to a difficult word. She sounds out the words carefully.

Lillis Rae is sitting again at the table and only the curve of her spine against the chair is visible to Stace. Occasionally a foot, bent back under the chair, taps an erratic rhythm, or an elbow flashes into sight past the frame of the door.

Stace stares out the window at the night sky, thinking back to that June morning.

He had parked the car on the shoulder of the road and he had sat there in the car with the sun coming up over the rim of the world, the clouds shining like beaten silver from below, light reflected up from the great swath of prairie. Through the screen of willows in the ditch he watched the house. This is probably the last I will see of her, he had thought. A face in a window, the movement of curtains behind glass. He had sat there for a minute more and realised he didn't want to think anymore. He wanted to feel nothing. He turned the key in the ignition and pulled the car around hard in the middle of the road and started back for the highway. The inside of the car smelling of goldenrod. On the back seat, a sleeping bag and an army surplus stuff sack with his clothes. He turned on the radio. He was leaving behind everything of his old life. He wouldn't think of her. She was already in the past now, getting further from him every moment.

The scrape of a chair on kitchen linoleum.

This beer's gone right through me, Tanya says, her voice clear to him down the hall, through the closed door. Back in a minute, she says. Footsteps down the hall toward him.

He steps over the side into the tub and Tanya opens the door and fumbles for the light switch. She closes the door partway and unzips her jeans.

If there's no soap by the sink there's a new bar on the edge of the tub you can use, Lillis Rae calls from the kitchen.

Thanks, Tanya says through the door. She flips up the toilet seat, pulling her underwear down to her knees as she turns to sit on the toilet. Christ, she says quietly to herself. She spools a length of paper from the roll and wraps it around her hand. She rocks forward over her bare thighs and clasps her ankles, resting her forehead on her knees, toilet paper wound like a bandage around her fingers. What am I doing, she says softly, to the floor between her feet.

She finishes peeing and stands to hitch her pants up. She bends over the tub and takes the bar of soap from the dish and almost touches Stace. She turns on the water and leans against the sink, looking at herself in the mirror. She flares her lips, peering at her gums.

You got any aspirin? she calls out. She opens the medicine cabinet and looks inside. I got a wicked headache coming on, she says.

I might have some upstairs, Lillis Rae says from the kitchen. Check the cabinet in there first.

I'm looking, Tanya says. I don't see any.

She presses the medicine cabinet door closed and glances in the mirror and sees Stace standing behind her.

What the fuck? She reaches up and puts her fingertips to the mirror, touches his reflection in the surface of the mirror, turns quickly to look at him but sees nothing.

He pushes aside the shower curtain and steps out of the tub to the bathroom floor. He stands in the bright, shabby bathroom and does not know what to do with his hands.

Tanya looks back into the mirror and sees him reflected there.

Don't, she whispers, her voice brittle, shrinking against the door frame. Don't. Her face white and drained of blood. She backs through the open door and closes it hard behind her.

This is what he sees from the corner of his eye: a face no longer his own in a mirror, a bleached photograph.

What's the matter? Lillis Rae calls from the kitchen.

He tries the door. Tanya is holding the handle from the other side. Through the door he can hear her breathing, harsh, as if she has run a marathon.

Nothing, Tanya says. Nothing.

What's going on? Lillis Rae comes down the hall and he sees her shadow in the gap beneath the door. You're shaking, Lillis Rae says. What's the matter?

Don't go in there, Tanya says. Don't go in there.

You look white as a sheet. You okay?

Tanya says nothing.

I'll get some aspirin from upstairs, Lillis Rae says. Sit down in the living room and I'll go get them.

Lillis Rae, this is going to sound crazy, okay, Tanya says, but I just saw Stace in your bathroom. I looked into the mirror and he was right there, for a second. He was right there in the room with me.

You're joking, right? Lillis Rae says.

No.

You just saw Stace in my bathroom?

He was standing in the tub, watching me. I was looking in the mirror and I saw him and then I turned around and he was gone.

You're creeping me out, Lillis Rae says. Let's have a drink and just calm down.

I'm sorry, Tanya says. I'm sorry.

Come on, Lillis Rae says, coaxing her from the door. We'll leave the bathroom closed and go sit in the kitchen.

He watches their shadows under the door as they move away down the hall toward the kitchen.

I don't know what happened, Tanya says. I'm sorry.

He opens the door and steps out into the hallway, closes the door. Tanya is sitting in the kitchen, her head dropped into her hands, holding her head up with her hands.

It's just a headache, Tanya says, her voice muffled. I'll be fine.

Lillis Rae takes two drinking glasses and the bottle of whiskey and sets them on the table.

Jesus christ, I need a smoke, she says, opening Tanya's pack of cigarettes. Mind if I bum one? Without waiting for an answer she lights a cigarette from the pilot light on the stove, sits again at the table to stare speculatively at the bottle of whiskey.

I didn't know you smoked, Tanya says, raising her head.

Lillis Rae's eyes narrow as smoke drifts up from her mouth, nostrils. She coughs, waves the smoke away. I had a dream about Stace last night, she says. He was standing beside my bed, and I saw him very clearly. His face was thin, even thinner than when he was young, but he was older, a lot of creases around his mouth and eyes. He looked like his father. But his nose was different. I asked him and he told me he broke it in a fight. There was a stripe of moonlight across his face, which looked very white. I said to him, Lie down beside me, and when he moved away from the bed the bar of light slid down his back and he disappeared. I can still see his eyes, which were almost white in the moonlight. I can still see them.

She flicks the cigarette into the ashtray.

I must have known all the time, though it wasn't until I was sitting down this morning with a coffee that I really recognised him. I haven't dreamed about him for a while. I sat at the table and put my head down and I went over the dream.

Tanya takes the top off the bottle and pours a shot into a glass and hands the glass to Lillis Rae.

I don't know what I saw in there, Tanya says. It scared the shit out of me.

Lillis Rae takes the glass of whiskey and swirls the alcohol, staring into the glass.

I try not to think about him, she says. Whatever he did that day had nothing to do with me. Two people are always separate. Whatever we had between us is lost.

Tanya pours herself a rye, sets the bottle on the table.

For a second he was right there, Tanya says. I saw him in the mirror and I turned around and he was standing there. I could have touched him. He was wearing some kind of white coveralls.

Lillis Rae pushes her chair back, stands with the glass. I kept all our photographs, she says. I looked back through some albums today. I looked back to see if I could figure out where it came from. What I saw in him.

She comes down the hallway toward him and he presses against the wall. She brushes past and he follows her into the living room. From the bottom of a bookcase she pulls two photo albums. She sits on the couch, opens them on the coffee table.

I'm wiped, Tanya calls from the kitchen. I think I'm going to go.

Stay, Lillis Rae says, without looking up from the photo albums. Bring the rye in here and look at pictures with me.

I can't, Tanya says. I'm kind of fucked up. I need to get some sleep. I didn't sleep hardly at all last night.

You okay to drive?

I'll be fine, Tanya says.

Tanya is standing with her coat and the bag of books in the kitchen, looking down the dark hall to the living room.

I'll call you next week, she says, putting her hand on the door handle.

There is no response from the living room.

Tanya opens the back door and steps out into the night.

VIDEO

She peels back the clear plastic sheet and lifts the photograph from the album.

Like a perfect lens, the air brings his face close to her. So she can see with amazing clarity all the details of his face as she has never seen them before. Or noticed before. Isn't only the light. She's sure it isn't the light. Maybe it's the alcohol.

She lays the photograph on the coffee table and picks up the remote control, hits the 'play' button. The TV screen goes blue, the word Video flashing white in the corner of the screen. Then the picture starts.

The sky is lit up from below by a luminous swell of snow that makes everything—even his face—silver. A cloud spills shadow across the field toward them, the sky and the land darkening to the colour of a photograph coming up under developer, everything still except the light, his face tilting up to look out the window, the window rolled down and his gloved hand on the dashboard. A small mole like a dark velvet match head under his skin, at the base of his ear. The skin behind his ear red and irritated by the scarf, his cheek stubbled. It looks like he has not shaven for a few days. In this beautiful light nothing is hidden. He smiles and turns to look into the lens.

You want a mandarin orange? he asks the camera. The fruit glows in the stiff leather folds of his glove.

She adjusts focus, the picture jumping and blurring and then coming in sharp on his face.

No. Her own voice, too loud, too close to the video camera's microphone.

I fucking love mandarin oranges, he says. I want to buy a whole case of mandarins every year in the winter. Ten pounds. Bundle up the skins in the little green papers, then put them back in the box. I want to keep the whole case on the seat next to me when I'm driving. They smell so good. I think I eat them for the smell.

He takes off the gloves to peel the orange, dropping narrow sections of fruit into his mouth.

Can you see this? he asks, holding a hand up to the camera. Can you get this close? Look at my nails. They're stained orange. From the peels.

He drops coin-shaped peels of orange into the green paper wrapper on the seat.

Roll up the window, she says, behind the camera. It's getting too cold in here.

He opens a thermos and sips coffee from the plastic lid, steam hanging between them in the frozen air.

It was almost springtime, and for once there was no wind. They sat together in the car and looked down over the bluff and below them in the distance the silver line of ice on the reservoir was visible between the trees. Light flared off the windscreen and Stace, out of the frame, said something that she couldn't make out, had never been able to decipher no matter how many times she rewound and replayed the video. Then the picture ends and she hits the 'stop' button and there is a blank blue screen again.

Fuck you, she says, thickly. She leans forward and knocks the albums off the coffee table, a pile of loose photographs scattering across the carpet. These are memories from some other lifetime, she thinks.

Lillis Rae contemplates her heart. It is, she decides, a room with several doors. It is Stace's architecture that shaped her heart — a room he always moved through awkwardly, hesitantly. His hands blind in her, searching for levers, devices, entrance and exit, his hands on her body at night, feeling his way through her heart, missing always the still centre, the quiet point around which she revolves. It is not him I feel inside me now, she thinks.

She takes a drink of whiskey, a long one, presses the tips of her fingers to her temples.

ASLEEP

IN THE BLUE WASH of the TV screen he watches her.

Lillis Rae is crying in her sleep. In her head, some fine mechanism has been destroyed. Blood hammers in a hidden cavity.

Despair coils in his chest. His lungs no longer lungs but collapsed bellows. Dead air refusing exhalation; poison, gas-like, penetrating the deepest fibres. He looks at his awkward blue hands. There are no answers there.

He closes his eyes and hears somewhere out in the night a freight train, the distant shriek of steel on steel.

He gets up out of the chair and opens the curtains a crack, switches off the TV. For a second everything vanishes, leaving only the floor under his feet, the centre of his vision black and then the sofa and the room fading slowly in. The air is flat and still, as if something has been lost. On the coffee table a photograph with the bottle of whiskey on it. In the semi-dark, the photograph is grey.

He moves the empty bottle aside and tilts the photograph up toward the window, examining it a moment before laying it face down on the coffee table.

He looks down at Lillis Rae, asleep on the sofa, at her strong thinness, her legs moving under the blanket, one leg opening and closing against the other like the action of a jackknife. She is sleeping on her side, a blanket and a sweater twisted around her shoulders, one fist on the cushion next to her cheek. A palm concealed within the fist. He sits on the edge of the sofa, touches her leg through the blanket, puts his mouth to the ear of the sleeping woman. She stirs lightly beneath him.

He says: Do not awake from sleep. Only in this dream can you hear me.

He pulls the blanket down and, rolling Lillis Rae onto her back, slides his arm under her and lifts her until she is sitting upright on the sofa. Her head lolls, drunk with sleep, to the side. She slumps back into the corner, her breath warm and sour with alcohol and smoke.

Sit up, he says. Come on. He folds her arms around her front, pulls the sweater around her shoulders. She sits there, swaying slightly on the sofa, her eyes closed, still dreaming.

On the coffee table three empty bottles of beer and the fifth of rye. A curtain breathes in then out like a membrane in a draft.

Lillis Rae, he says. Can you hear me?

The woman dips her chin. Yes, she mumbles.

Open your eyes.

She looks to his voice, opens her eyes, focuses slowly on the dim figure beside her.

Do you recognise me? he asks in the darkness.

Lillis Rae says nothing.

You know who I am, he says. In the wan light filtering through the curtains his face is deeply lined, thin, the contours of skull barely disguised. It's Stace, he says.

She lets a small cry curl out from her throat, her hand coming up instinctively to touch the side of his face.

He catches hold of her wrist, massaging the inside of her arm with his thumb, moves closer to her on the sofa. Lillis Rae shakes her head, turns and lays her head against his shoulder.

Perhaps it is all a mystery. The confused instinct of limbs, corroded wires in her head and chest. She is touching him now as if she knows what she is doing. Dreaming she is awake. He imagines it is often like this: a photograph; a ring concealed in the top drawer of her dressing table; a word. Memories hidden in her body like tiny triggers.

He will uncover the story as she must know it, in fragments and unclearly. It is he who walks through her sleep with his arms swinging from the hinges of his shoulders.

Are you still with me? he asks.

Lillis Rae turns her head, closes her eyes.

Look at me, he says. Who is it you see?

It's Stace, she says, without turning her head or opening her eyes. She moves her tongue thickly. It's Stace come back to see me, she says. She rubs her thighs with the palms of her hands, as if to resuscitate numb flesh.

Gently, with the tips of his fingers, Stace turns her face back to him. Can you see me? he asks.

Yes, she says.

You cannot see me, Stace says. I touch you now, and you feel nothing. I speak, and it is only your imagination, spinning slow like a wheel in the dark.

She says nothing.

He says, Tell me your dream.

We're crossing a river, she says. The cables belly into the wind and I don't know if we're still moving, though the deck is vibrating under my feet. Everyone is out of their cars, looking over the railing. A big tree has snagged one of the cables in the water, and the ferry is in the middle of the river, unable to either advance or return. Two men using long metal poles try to push the tree away from the cable, but the current is too strong, and they give up. People go back to their cars and wait. The captain stands in his shirt sleeves talking into a radio. No one seems upset about the delay. Finally someone in a motorboat comes out to the ferry with a chainsaw to cut us loose. A few people lean over the railing to watch. The motorboat bangs against the hull of the ferry right underneath me.

I look down into the brown seethe of the river. It is you in the boat with the chainsaw. You manoeuvre the small boat until you are close enough to the roots of the tree to start cutting, but then you kneel in the bottom of the boat and look into the water. A naked foot is wedged in a tangle of roots, barely above the swirling water. You glance up at me to see if I too have seen it. You reach down into the water and with difficulty unhook the leg from the tree, and whatever you have hold of is so heavy the boat is nearly capsized when the current drags at it. Brown water slops into the bottom of the motorboat. You succeed in pulling the thing up against the side of the boat, and little by little manage to lift it from the suck of the river until in a flail of limbs it rolls into the boat, and there is the flash of a ragged white face that I do not recognise. You cover it with a sheet and crouch in the bottom of the boat. Hiding it from us. But I saw it. No one from the ferry is saying anything.

The people at the railing have their backs to the river and are reading maps, instruction manuals, or smoking.

Of course, she says, I remember there was never a ferry across the river.

Beneath the floor, the furnace in the basement kicks on, and he can feel it in his feet through the carpet.

I have something for you, he says. He takes Lillis Rae's hand, rests it on his thigh. Slips the ring onto her finger. Do you remember this ring? He holds her hand up in front of her face, strokes the silver band.

In the top drawer of her dresser, where it had always been kept, he had found the cloisonné jewelry box. He had spilled the contents on the dresser, spread the tangle of earrings and necklaces until he found the ring. A thin band of engraved silver. His ring.

Lillis Rae does not respond, staring mutely at the dark ceiling.

Stace puts thumb and forefinger under her chin, tilts her head to look at him. The ring, he says. Can you see the ring?

Yes, she says.

He leans back, releasing her jaw.

She has turned her face to the window. Her breathing slowing now until she takes her hand from his, dries her cheek.

I want you to tell me whose ring is on your hand, Stace says.

She rubs her thumb over the engraved initials, turns her hand, turns the ring up to the light. I kept it for you in case you changed your mind, she says.

Changed my mind about what?

I kept it for when you decided to come back, Lillis Rae says.

SUNDAY MORNING EARLY 5

ROADBLOCK

IT WAS THE COIL WIRE, Wes says. Somehow the fucking wire got unplugged from the distributor.

He is sitting in front of the TV with his sock feet one on either side of the screen, and he has a knife in his lap and he is whittling something out of a piece of wood. On the floor between his legs is a pile of white shavings. I fixed the truck, he says.

Tanya closes the door and leans against it, puffs a strand of hair from her face. I felt like puking the whole time I was there, she says. I shouldn't have gone.

You didn't have to go, Wes says without looking up, brushing curls of wood from his lap. She probably could have used a night off.

She pushes away from the door and comes into the room and falls back onto the bed without undoing her coat. She stares blankly at the ceiling. It would have been odd if I didn't go, she says. I haven't missed a session in about six months. She folds an arm over her eyes, drops her bag onto the bed.

So how did it go? You learn how to spell 'alibi' tonight?

Don't give me any shit, she says wearily. Let's just get this over with, alright, Mr. Fixit?

How the fuck you think I feel, Wes says, swinging his feet down from the TV. He folds the knife away, brushes off the front of his pants as he stands. I'm going nuts in here. Somebody peels back that tarpaulin for a look-see and we're fucked.

I saw Stace at Lillis Rae's place, she says, without moving her arm. I totally saw him. He was standing in her bathroom, standing in the tub, watching me take a pee.

Gimme a fucking break, Wes says, leaning to scoop up the pile of shavings. He grabs his boots and sits on the edge of the bed and jams his feet into the snakeskin boots, pulling hard on the side tabs. He pulls his jeans over the tops and stomps his heels deeper into the boots.

I gotta get the fuck out of here before you lose it completely. This crazy shit is not part of the game plan.

Lillis Rae wanted to talk about him.

You talked about him? For chrissakes!

Tanya sits up on the bed, searches in her purse and pulls out a lighter and a fresh pack of cigarettes. She strips the cellophane off and drops it on the bedspread.

Lillis Rae said she had a dream about Stace last night. It must have been right around the time he was dying.

I dream all the time, Wes says. It doesn't mean a goddamn thing.

He was wearing white coveralls, Tanya says. Zip-up coveralls with a floppy neck.

Wes pulls on his jacket. You ready?

As ready as I'm going to be, I guess, Tanya says without moving from the bed, blowing smoke up into his face.

Wes looks at the television. The bar closed an hour ago. Parking lot should be cleared out by now. You go down ahead and take a look. I'll go out the back and walk around the end of the motel.

He reaches under the mattress and takes the keys for the red truck, bounces the magnet box once in the palm of his hand before he drops it in his pocket.

Then let's go, he says. Get your ass in gear.

Tanya puts the cigarette in her mouth and takes a long drag, not taking her eyes off his face. Then she gets up without a word and brushes past him and stubs the cigarette out in the overflowing ashtray on the table. She takes the plastic flask from the purse, unscrews the top, and takes a swig. She glances at herself in the mirror above the table, touches the corners of her mouth with a fingertip.

What're you looking at? she asks.

I'm waiting for you, Wes says, looking at her reflection in the mirror.

I appreciate you cleaning up those wood shavings, she says.

Outside, the sky is hazy and soft in the sodium glow of the lights and the red truck is powdered with new snow. The bar, a long, low cinder block building, lit now only by neon beer signs, is quiet and dark, the parking lot out front deserted. Across the street an autobody shop is a windowless cube, and inside, behind big metal doors, a dog barks twice.

Wes holds one hand out, palm upturned, to the snow. Can't see worth shit in this weather, he says. Sure wish it wasn't snowing. Then again, maybe it's a good thing.

It's not that bad, Tanya says, looking up at the sky. I like driving in the snow. Bob put all season radials on my car last winter.

Tracks, Wes says. If it's going to snow, I want a lot of snow to cover our tracks.

It was snowing out at Lillis Rae's place. The TV said it's going to snow the rest of the weekend, Tanya says. She pulls the collar of her coat across her throat, holds it closed. It's not supposed to be too cold. They said it'd be minus eight or so by morning.

Let's hit the road, he says. You follow me in your car.

He watches her cross the parking lot to her car. Icicle lights have already been strung outside the lobby, and decorative aerosol snow sprayed into the corners of windows. Propped against the glass of the office is a snow shovel and a sack of rock salt.

He takes a bank card from his wallet and stretches up over the hood of the truck and with the card scrapes the windshield and side window clean, knurls of icy snow spraying out from under the edge of the plastic.

He takes the keys out of his pocket and opens the truck. He climbs in and slams the door. His breath in the cab like ice smoke. He says a silent prayer and the truck starts immediately. He turns on the heat. Through the blurry side window he sees her brake lights flash and then her back-up lights and she eases the car out of her stall and idles, waiting for him. He lets the truck warm for a moment, tilting the air against the windows, a patch clearing above the steering wheel. Tanya waves at him from her car, mouths, Let's go.

He puts the truck in gear and pulls away from the curb, swinging past the bar and out onto the access road, taking it slow past the all night service station, her headlights in his rearview mirror. The light is green as he turns onto the highway and she makes it through the intersection with him on a yellow, and they are the only two vehicles on the road. The air blows warm and he opens the top of his jacket, holding his collar between his teeth and pulling at the zipper with a gloved hand. On the surface of the highway snow skates and drifts under the headlights. He switches the radio on to a country station.

At the reservoir they hit the roadblock with no warning. The car he has been following suddenly stabs on its brakes and ahead he sees the blue and red lights flashing against the trees. He rounds the curve and there is nowhere to go. He pumps the brakes and Tanya's car slows behind him but it is too late. It is right at the t-intersection where he had planned to turn off behind the reservoir. On the shoulder, two cruisers are parked nose to tail, rotating beacon lights twirling silently, and the car ahead of him stops and the driver rolls down the side window. A cop in a parka and reflective vest leans briefly into the car and says something to the driver and then stands away from the car. The car pulls ahead and then does a tight u-turn in the road and comes back toward Wes. The cop makes a circling 'come here' motion with his flashlight and Wes rolls the truck forward, lowering his window. Grey flakes flare over the windshield.

What the fuck. He can feel nervous sweat prickling at his armpits, and his stomach contracts like he is going to be sick.

Road's closed, the cop calls as he approaches the truck. There is snow in his hair and moustache. He is carrying a long rubberized flashlight in one hand and a radio in the other.

Looking through the sweep of the wipers, Wes can see three ambulances parked sideways across the road, and beyond them, behind barricades, a big diesel auto wrecker with its boom work lights shining down onto the black water of the reservoir. A mud-streaked Lincoln Continental has been chained up on the flatbed, water draining from the underside of the car, the husk of the drowned car skinned with ice so it glows yellow under the arc lights. Men are clustered at the winch controls, the crane swung out over the reservoir, a cable with a hook suspended above the smoking surface of the water. In the water a rigid inflatable boat with the word Police stenciled on the pontoons. Two divers in drysuits are staring down into the water off to the side of the boat, the water lit from below by a powerful lamp.

On the shoulder of the road, ambulance attendants unfold a black body bag between them. Squatting at their feet, another pair of workers are quickly zipping a bag around the third of the five bodies laid out on sheets, the two remaining incongruously barefoot, clad only in soaking T-shirts and jeans.

The diesel is growling and water is springing off the taut cable and he sees the divers have attached a line to the hook. The lighted water boils gold and then a webbed stretcher rises and breaks the surface, water pouring through the stretcher as it rises and spins slowly through the air. On the stretcher a long, man-shaped package wrapped in algae-green plastic, three weed-clogged cinder blocks strapped against the package. Above the noise of the engine he hears shouts from the men standing in the boat. One of them has a gaff pole and he is hooking something in the water.

The cop puts a gauntleted hand on Wes's door.

Highway's closed, he says to Wes through the open window. You'll have to turn around and use an alternate route tonight.

No problem, officer, Wes says. Looks like you got your hands full.

We got a car in the reservoir, the cop says, looking down the bank. Didn't make the corner it looks like.

The crane swings in over the road with the stretcher and a cop guides it to the ground beside the other bodies. The rear doors of one of the ambulances open and a woman in a parka jumps down and walks with a camera to the stretcher, crouching to photograph the plastic-swathed thing under the floodlights.

The cop's radio barks again and he puts it up to his mouth and mutters something.

Headlights cut across Wes's face, and in the rearview mirror he sees Tanya has turned her car around behind him and is pulling away from the roadblock.

Okay, the cop says, tapping Wes's door panel with the butt of the flashlight. Turn around and go back about ten minutes and you'll find an intersection. You'll make a wide swing around this whole section of highway. Let's go before we cause another accident. You drive safe. He waves the flashlight in a tight circle.

Wes rolls up his window and eases forward.

Dickey, he thinks, looking at the shrouded figure on the stretcher. So there's Dickey. And in the back of the truck, close enough that he could touch him if he were to put his arm out the rear window of the cab, Stace with his postcard, explaining all.

He turns the truck around and follows Tanya's taillights. They drive for five minutes before he flashes his high beams and puts on his signal light, the roadblock lost behind them in the night. Tanya pulls over onto the shoulder of the highway, puts her hazard flashers on. He parks the truck and gets out and she leans over and unlocks the passenger door as he crosses behind her car.

Un-*fucking*-believable, he says, getting in, putting his hands heavily on his knees.

I was shitting bricks, she says. I didn't know what was going on. I thought there was an APB out on the truck. I thought it was a roadblock.

We gotta get rid of the fucking truck, Wes says. He punches a gloved hand against the dash.

I couldn't see them very well, Tanya says. They looked like kids. Just kids.

It wasn't only the kids, Wes says, his voice tight. Did you see who they just pulled out of the reservoir with the crane?

I'm no good at guessing, Tanya says.

Take a wild guess.

I don't know. Dickey?

Bingo.

There's a new mickey behind your seat, she says. Pass it over.

I could even see the three cinder blocks, Wes says, reaching behind the seat.

Christ.

Exactly, he says.

So we can't drop Stace at the reservoir. That's out. It's just like he wrote on the postcard.

Definitely one hundred percent out, Wes says. I just hope the cop doesn't remember the truck.

Then Plan B, Tanya says. We go to Plan B.

Wes stares out through the windshield into the night. Right, Plan B, he says.

So what's Plan B? Tanya asks, opening the mickey.

Above the burr of the car's heater they hear the train, the distant arcing call of the whistle, and then the engines hammer past out of the night, snow driving and whirling into the blast of headlamps. The sound of diesel powerplants beating like a giant heart inside the car. They watch the train go past, sparks striking off steel, the double-quick *thun-thun* of wheels down the long line of boxcars and then the red lamps of the caboose and dark again.

Wes takes the bottle and screws the cap on and puts the plastic mickey bottle under his seat.

They sit in silence and the windows fog over and after awhile Tanya punches the dash lighter and lights another cigarette.

There's empty houses out at Lillis Rae's new subdivision, she says at last. Maybe we should drive out that way. Take him home, sorta.

BREAK-IN

FILAMENTS OF ICE come up like wrought silver leaf on the window by his head. With the thumb of his glove he burns a hole through the frost and looks out past the show homes. Across the empty field he can see the distant break of shadowy trees, and beyond that, almost invisible to him in the snow and the dark, Lillis Rae's house, the faint glow of her yard light. She will be asleep, and see none of this in the night. Wes sits for a minute in the dark cab, feeling wind buffet the truck, rocking it on its suspension. He lets out a breath then and opens the door and steps down with one foot to the running board, hoists himself up the side of the truck and into the box without touching the ground. He squats in the bottom of the truck box and lifts the tarpaulin away and it snaps in the wind, coming back down over his arms. He tucks a corner of the tarp under one of the bungie cords and wrestles Stace's body until he has both legs out from under and he can see Stace's hiking boots. Wes takes off his gloves and kneels, working quickly at the laces in the dark, stops to blow on his fingers to warm them. He unlaces the boots and gets them off Stace's feet and removes his own cowboy boots, slips his feet into Stace's icy boots. The boots fit. He jams the laces into the top of the hikers and puts his gloves on, stands his own boots aside. He folds the tarp as best he can, jams it into a space behind the cab so it won't blow away. He reaches over and drops open the tailgate and then swings back over the front of the truck box to the running board, jumps to the ground. The snow comes up over the tops of Stace's hiking boots.

He walks up the driveway of the middle house and up the front steps and peers in the living room window. Light from the streetlamp shows him a bare white room, a table saw set up in the centre of the room where one day a dining room suite will be placed. He tries the door. Locked.

  He goes back down the steps and around the side where he finds the door into the garage is unlocked. He crosses through the garage and lets himself into the house. Inside, it's warm, a furnace roaring in the basement. He walks through empty rooms, looks out the living room window to the red truck parked in front of the dumpster. His tracks on the driveway already drifting over. Out on the road he can see Tanya's car where she waits for him.

He climbs into the back of the truck and pulls Stace by the legs toward him. Stace is frozen in a fetal position. He gets one arm under Stace's knees and the other behind the neck and picks Stace up in a fireman's lift from the tailgate of the truck. Up close, Wes sees the ridges of the truckbed liner have imprinted a debossed pattern on the side of Stace's cheek. Stace's eyelashes, the hair in his nostrils, white with frost. With difficulty Wes hoists the body up over his shoulder and, carrying Stace like an oversize sack of flour, staggers up the driveway to the show home, pushes through the side door. He leans against a wall to rest, taking Stace's weight on his thighs. Under his coat he is drenched in sweat. After a minute he gets his breath back and he hitches Stace up into his arms again and manoeuvres him down the hallway and into the front room. In the living room, Wes backs down a wall until he can kneel to lay the body on the floor. The room is fragrant with sawdust.

Wes straddles the still body. Stace's eyes are open, staring at the pile of sawdust beneath the table saw. From a pocket, Wes takes the used syringe and the crumpled foil packet, lays them on the floor next to Stace's outstretched hand.

He sits back and removes the hikers, laces one boot onto Stace's foot, leaving the other aside as if it has been kicked off his bare foot. He stands in the room. His socks are wet and leave foot-shaped prints on the plywood sub-floor when he walks out of the house.

A kilometre away, headlights swing low across the trees and the field, distant trees printing against the darkness like fine bones on an x-ray.

His cowboy boots in hand, Wes walks in sock feet through the ankle-deep snow around to the back of Tanya's car and opens the trunk. The hooded red light pops on. He jams the blanket behind the spare tire and drops the trunk lid.

He gets into the car. The empty bottle slides under the seat. In the rearview mirror he watches the headlights approach, a band of light sliding across his face. He leans across the seat, taking Tanya by the shoulder and pulling her upright. Come on you bitch, he says. Wake up. He lowers her dead weight against his chest, resting his chin on the top of her cold skull. One slack arm he raises and folds across his own chest. Tanya slumps against him, murmuring something he cannot make out. He kisses the part of her hair. Help me out here, he whispers, pressing his lips into limp hair. As the car nears, their two shadows are thrown by the headlights against the inside of the iced windshield for a moment, and then the yellow Lincoln goes past in a rattle of gravel and snow, a girl leaning out the passenger window of the car, her face white and strained. A bottle explodes and vanishes in the black wake of the car.

He sits in darkness, holding the sleeping woman, who does not move in his arms.

SUNDAY MORNING EARLY 6

SHOTGUN

WAKE UP.

When he opens his eyes Lillis Rae is standing just inside the kitchen door, looking down at him, her face cut in half by shadow. The shotgun held against her leg.

Wake up, she says.

Stace sits up in the chair. The clock above the stove shows several hours have passed. He must have slept and yet he feels drunk with fatigue.

You were asleep on the couch, he says groggily. I've been waiting for you.

How long has she been standing there in the doorway, watching him? The conversation starting as if she has been waiting for him to simply return to the house and pull up a chair in her head.

Something woke me, she says. I saw you there at the table, and for a moment I didn't know what to do. I thought I might kill you.

He tries to clear his head. Concentrate. In his mind he had seen it all perfectly. How it would happen. It was like watching a movie. And now it is happening and he is in it and nothing hangs together as it should. Unspooling out of control. He raises a hand to his face and his hand is shaking as if with palsy. He doesn't know even himself anymore. What was at the centre, what was familiar, is empty. What they thought they knew about each other—all that has changed. It seems almost impossible for this to have happened, and yet there is also a feeling of inevitability to it. They have arrived here, in this room, like strangers.

She comes into the kitchen.

I guess you're making yourself at home, she says.

The door was unlocked, he says.

She breaks open the shotgun, jacks the shells out into her hand, places the stubby red shells on the counter. Lays the gun down on the counter, the nickel-plate barrel scraping the edge of the sink.

What kind of trouble are you in this time?

She looks at him and he sees her eyes are hollowed and bloodshot and rimmed with red as if from crying. Perhaps the room is too bright. Light bleaching all colour out of his hands, his haggard face reflected in the kitchen window. She has been crying. He remembers the sound of her and it cuts into him, the knowledge. But what has been done is done, he thinks, to calm himself. The past an unstable territory.

She opens the door to the fridge. Swigs milk from an open bottle. Stares into the open fridge at wilting vegetables.

She puts her hand softly to the side of the humming fridge, notices for the first time the ring on her finger.

She knocks the fridge closed with an elbow. Runs the tap and takes a mug from the draining board and pours herself water. Her teeth aching with cold. Something like a knife pressing at the back of her eyes. She wipes her fingers on the side seam of her jeans, giving herself time to think.

In this dream a woman she recognises as herself walks along the overgrown depression of a dry, abandoned slough. Weeds drag at her bare legs, insects spinning up like small particles of glass. A man walks ahead of her, bending the branches of poplars out of her path. She watches his back. The man stumbles, trips on a small wooden box half-buried in the ground. Impatiently, he moves on. Bending down to examine the find, she calls to the man to stop, come back, wait, but he pushes on through the brush, until his blue shirt is lost in the tangle of trees.

The box is caked with mud, though she can see a line where a lid has been snugly fitted into the top of the box. Using a twig, she scrapes hardened mud from the box until the lid can be opened. Inside the box is a head. The face at first seems to be that of a stranger. Its eyes are open, watching her. She reaches without fear into the box and gently pries open the mouth. A ring falls into her hand. She takes the ring and closes the box. As she stands up the box sinks slowly into the ground until the earth has closed smoothly over it. Beneath her feet, the mysterious head moves through earth, turning, sinking.

It is only now she realises it is Stace's face she has seen in the box, asleep beneath the trees.

What're you doing in my house? she asks.

His wife in the middle of the room, a glass of water in her hand as she turns to look at him.

For a moment, Stace believes he can stop breathing.

It seems to have drained out of him, leaving him mute at the table. The deeper he goes, the less he knows. Inside, quicksand. They have stayed always on the edges of each other, where it is safe. *I know you*, he had said when she asked. *I know you. I've been inside you, as deep as anyone can go*, he had said, but it was still just the edge. He had concentrated on a few surface details: the shape of her lip, the curve of a breast, an arm, scars he or someone else put there, the soft scruff at the back of a neck, incoherent memories of a time spent at some campground, fucking against the side of a car in a mountain parking lot, her sweet, warm breath at the corner of his eye—that is what and how he knows her. In the dark her body a map he could trace and retrace with five or six always-repeated routes. Hidden currents driving her muscles and it had had nothing to do with him. No memories, no history, nothing that he knew.

I've come back to you, he says. I've come back but I can't stay here. His pulse tolling.

She pulls out a chair, sits at the table across from him. Her hand trembling almost invisibly, her face barely together. But her eyes are hard, locking onto him, holding him there, waiting for him to speak. As if it were possible to answer such a question. She puts the mug on the table, carefully, cradles it against her palm, two fingers through the handle and around the side.

How to answer? His mouth a blank. There is a reason he is here, he is certain, but nothing will fix. The perfect spool of the film unwinding. All his reasons leave the room, leaving her here. He is looking down at her from the ceiling. The air tilting precariously between them.

Their relationship with each other so complicated and yet so simple that they have spent years getting to know what they recognised in the first five minutes. To come back to themselves, and find the other still there, or already long departed. As is the case.

Like everything, this realization comes too late.

I saw you at the table and thought you were a stranger, she says. I wish you had been. You've come back and now even hope is gone. There's nothing left of us for you to destroy. I once knew you — thought I did — but I don't know you anymore. You left me and you changed, you've grown away. You're someone other than the person I loved.

She looks at him, searching his face. Looking for him. Folds her hand over his, bending his fingers under into a fist until the skin goes white across her knuckles. Nails dig into the palm of his hand.

I thought this might happen, she says. You returning from wherever it is you went, something torn out of the centre of you, something I loved. Yet I hoped it would be possible to reach that same place again, with enough patience, with time. That place we used to share.

I thought about you a lot. Almost always at first, after you left. I talked to you in my mind. Everything about you was so clear. We'd have long conversations when you got back from wherever it was you had gone to. For a long time I could pretend you were coming back to me. I could feel you walking around in my head. I never suspected you wouldn't come back. That you wouldn't come back for me. To me.

First your face went. I knew it was you I was talking to, but you were a blur. When I looked at a photograph I tried to mould the face to yours in my head. Or the other way around. The few photographs I have of you are from long ago, and picture you much younger than the night you left, and I had trouble connecting the face in the photographs to the shape of the man I talked to. It was as if a light shining on you left your face, head, in shadow.

Some mornings I would wake up and know you had spoken my name out loud, woken me to tell me something. I would feel some important message had been almost delivered—a vital bit of information, such as where you were, when you were returning—and then lost at the last moment. When I woke up I hoped I would remember what the voice had said, but I was unable to. Trying to sink into the same piece of sleep, to recapture the words. When your voice went I don't know. I can't remember. But one day I realised it was not your voice I could hear but my own. Then I knew I had truly lost you. It wasn't until I sat down here now that I realised there's nothing left between you and me. It has all been used up. Like air.

She lifts her fingers away from his hand. She says, What was I waiting for? The first moment, the first touch, and I know I'm missing all the things I once knew. I wish I knew nothing at all. I hate you.

There are two things to settle, she says. The first thing is Dickey. I don't want to know what it is you've done. It doesn't matter anymore. The past is all hypothetical. I think you killed him and that's all I need to know. You have that in you and I want no part of it. They found his boy at the reservoir and the empty rowboat and the Jeep, but never Dickey. And I think it's safe to say you know exactly what happened that day. You carried the boy out of our house to your car and that was the last I saw of you. Standing beside your car with your army bag and the boy in the carrier seat. You left me here in this house, haunted by memories, and it was as if our history meant nothing to you.

Once I almost wrote a letter to the police, telling them what I knew. Then I realised I knew nothing about you.

The second thing I want to know is why you're here. Why you've come back. Why now?

You used to ask me if I loved you, Stace says. And I would reply, Of course. How much? you'd ask. With everything in me, I'd say. And I'd spread my arms wide as I could, taking in the whole room. But I see now it wasn't all that much. There wasn't enough in me. I said the words so easily: *Love. Yes. Everything. Forever.* And yet I knew nothing. I wasn't paying attention to the words even as I said them. You heard me and tried to believe me and maybe you did believe me. I said I loved you and I was speaking of something else altogether.

When I thought of returning, sometimes I imagined that I would awaken in this very chair, he says. In this house with you. What happened with Dickey a part of the past that had been erased clean from my life. And I could never sustain that for more than an hour. I killed him and I betrayed you and I poisoned the whole past. Our life. There is never one single act of betrayal.

When I dreamt of you, most often we were making love. Now those dreams are less vivid. Once it was in the back of a car, perhaps at a drive-in movie. There was a voice coming over the radio speaker, talking to us. I could feel myself inside you, and I looked up into a huge face, a god-sized eye wrapped around the windshield, looking in at us and what we were doing to each other. We were so close we ignited each other. Even your skin turned to flame. Maybe it is enough to simply have felt that even once.

He says, Everything that happens between us now is untraceable. You will wake from this in the morning and find the ring on your finger and remember this conversation as a dream.

He raises a hand from the table, lets it fall gently on her sleeping arm. He reaches for her and then it is easy. The touch of her unlocking something in him. He looks at her and her skin is translucent and he sees her lit from within by the disease. Already the cells have formed in her a branching network of minute red filaments, a cluster rooted in her left breast, spreading through her chest and into her lungs. Filtering through flesh at a microscopic pace even as he watches, invading her tissues, the disease burning through her so slowly that she does not yet feel any pain and perhaps will not for years. And then it will be too late.

He closes his eyes and still he sees it at work inside her. This is my torture, he thinks: to see death within her and to be powerless to prevent it or to warn her.

She says, I can see a blue swimming pool, and beside it a small glass bottle filled with a bright green fluid. I don't know why I always think of that when I think of the night you left. I have the ring you gave me, though it doesn't fit my hand. Everything is a different size now. Things fit differently than they used to.

She wants to say something else, but cannot remember what it is.

You look like hell, she says finally.

He stands up unsteadily, puts his hands on her shoulders.

Don't, she says.

She turns up to look at him, and he bends over her and kisses her mouth from above. Her lips part under his mouth, her teeth knocking against his, their mouths open, questioning. Her eyes hazel, flecked with gold, staring upside down into his, amazed at the shocking intimacy of the thing, the kiss.

SCARS

THE ONLY THING to fear is silence. Everything is buried there.

Where are you now? Stace whispers. They are lying together on top of her bed. Her arms adrift on the blankets, forgotten, asleep. He founders on her body, his back broken over her as if on a shoal thrown up in the dark.

On the bed, he holds the sleeping woman still in his arms. In her the secret topography of desire. Like a lover, he can trace its paths over her skin. Closer. Breathing through her mouth. He is a shadow within her, passing through the spaces in her at another frequency. His fingers at the base of her brain. Dreaming is for those who sleep at night.

He touches her breast through the shirt.

There's a long room, Lillis Rae says. At first it's too dark to see clearly, but I can feel your hands on me. We're standing up against the wall. It feels like concrete against the back of my head. When I press my ear to the wall I can hear a motor running, and voices, though I can't hear what is said. When I take my head away from the wall there is a silence. You say, I want to move through you like blood. I want to hear your thoughts, every one. This is what I want. Exactly this. The things all lovers want.

When you say it, I want to look into your face, she says, but there is no light. It is always too dark inside a room to see you. You move inside me and no matter how deep you go you can't touch me all the way.

She puts her hand over his, where her heart should be. I've hidden it here, she says. The telltale heart. Beneath these ribs.

Tell me about your heart, he says.

She shakes her head. Sometimes I don't think there's much left. There's not a lot to say. Most of the time I feel nothing. Then something makes me think of you—maybe a dream, or the print of a boot heel in the dirt, a radio playing—and even then it's not a pain I feel but there is a trace, you know, even after so long. A hitch in me, and I'd know you are still out there, though a long way off, and the line was still connecting you and me. It's like a fish hooked deep inside, waiting at the bottom of the lake, too hurt to move, just floating there still and waiting with the hook in its guts, sending the tiniest tremors up the line.

I know I hurt you, he says. I'd do it differently if I could, but that's impossible.

Every time you touched me, you left a scar, Lillis Rae says. She pulls the bottom of her blue shirt from her jeans, twisting sideways on the bedclothes to display a fading pucker of scar at the base of her spine. Remember when I got this one? she asks.

No. Stace does not remember. He puts his fingers on her skin, feels the velvet knot of vertebrae. He moves his hand up her body, until he is under her shirt. Her naked breast cool beneath his touch. She says nothing.

He kisses her arm. The smell of clean cotton.

Lillis Rae sits up on the edge of the bed, leans forward to rest her elbows on her knees. With one hand she loosens her hair, shaking it out across her shoulders. I got that scar when we were cleaning trout by the lake, she says. You always liked cleaning trout—the guts smelled sweet to you when you opened them up. I never understood that. We were kneeling together in the shade of your father's boathouse. It must have been early summer, because the trailer for his motorboat was right there, behind us, and when I stood up from scaling a fish, the corner of the licence plate on the trailer got me right on the spine. You could see white gristle it cut so deep.

Stace runs his fingertips over the ridge of skin. Why didn't you get stitches?

Lillis Rae shakes her head. Too dangerous. Anaesthetic on the spine can paralyze you.

Stace slides his hand down the back of her jeans until the nub of her coccyx is under his fingers. Do you have other scars? he asks. He reaches under her arm, opens the top of her jeans.

There are others, she says. The scars are mine, not yours. Only I can read them. The one on the inside of my elbow is from the time we were making love in the back of the car, when my arm got stuck in the crack between the seats. Do you remember that?

No. Stace does not remember.

She kisses him, twice, on the eyes. Nothing that is left here belongs to you, she says.

He pulls her back against him so that she is lying across his chest, puts his mouth to the side of her throat. He runs his fingers through her hair, spreading it out strand by strand in a net over her face until she brushes it aside and brings her lips up to his, pushing her tongue into his mouth. They feed on the movement of lips which know exactly the patterns of pleasure. Blood tugging at the base of his cock. He presses against her hip, lifts a thigh over her, feeling his erection slide across the seam of her jeans.

She unbuttons the shirt, lets it fall away. Her shoulders burning against the mattress.

It's been a long time since I've been touched the way you're touching me now, she says.

He pushes the shirt off her shoulders, moves his hand down across her breasts, stops at her belly. Her breasts soft and elastic under his mouth.

Your hands are trembling, she says.

She traps his hand there, stroking the back of it with the ball of her thumb.

It's as if you are a perfect stranger, she says.

Stace kisses the hollow at the base of her throat where a vein pulses, letting his tongue trace small intimate patterns on her skin.

She closes her eyes, pushes his hand down her body.

They listen to the tick of a clock on the night table by the bed.

I think I may be dreaming, she says. She rolls off the bed, stepping out of her jeans, kicks them to the floor, lets her shirt fall away. Her legs white as clay as they go into dark work socks.

Are you going to undress? she asks.

No.

He turns over to look up at her.

Sit down here, he says, moving his legs on the bed. You'll get cold.

I want you to make love to me right now, before I change my mind, she says, lying half on top of him on the bed.

He rolls out from beneath her, kneeling on the bedroom floor, shifts her so that her legs are on either side of him. The soft inside of her thighs flaring where they press over the edge of the bed frame.

She pulls his mouth into her, tilting her pelvis up, hungry for his touch, the smell of her through cotton worn so thin he can see the swell and cleft of her pudendum. He puts his mouth to her, breathing through thin fabric until the cotton is damp and clinging with his breath. Her hands like wires holding him there between her thighs.

I've seen a friend, he works with me at the plant, she says. You wouldn't know him. We went out a few times. I don't know if I'll see him again. That was about four or five months ago. The first few times he blotted you out completely, but later I could feel you inside me again. I wish I knew what you meant to me.

The deep rift of her spine, arched under his hand. Stace kisses the soft flesh of her thighs, letting his tongue slip under the elastic of her underwear as she drags them down, spreads her pussy with two fingers. He bites gently at her hand, pushes the tip of his tongue past her knuckles and into her, his cock jammed against the side of the mattress through the white coveralls. He strains to reach deeper, finding the long channel inside her, as if he will consume her very flesh.

It's like a secret language, she whispers, her hands moving up and down his back, holding him against the heat of her skin.

She works her fingers into his hair, pulling him up until he is lying over her, blocking out all the light in the room. As she kisses him, the sweetness of honey. When she awakes in the morning the taste of something like honey on skin will float at the back of her mind.

*   *   *

When he enters her he tries to remember if it has happened before, but he remembers nothing. He is leaving behind everything of his old life. Losing even the names for things. It is as if he is a perfect stranger.

FIRST LIGHT

IT IS NEARING DAWN. The mirror a steel eye floating against the wall. Light pales the window above the bed.

He slides his hand beneath the sheet and touches her.

I've got to go, he says. I've been here long enough.

She rolls toward him without opening her eyes and holds his hand against her. What time is it?

Almost dawn, he says.

Is it dark still?

Yes, he says.

Last night I dreamed about you, she murmurs into the pillow.

You're still dreaming, he says.

He looks at Lillis Rae, her face given over to sleep.

It is impossible to know what is in her sleep, her body a question mark under the sheets.

He parts the curtains, leans on the window sill to look down into the grey, still yard. The dark face of a cat peering up at him from the flowerbed beneath the window.

At the far edge of the yard, among the wind-break of caraganas, Emmett stands spraddle-legged to urinate, hot piss steaming and foaming through the crust of last night's snow to black earth. Even from that distance Stace can see it is Emmett waiting for him and for a moment everything stammers drunken around him. Blood fluttering like a red curtain behind his eyes. The end of the story tattooed on the backs of his hands. As if now at the window he is able to see to the root of that which has driven him here.

Behind him, the woman asleep and going on without him. In her heart a light has gone out. Her dreams are blind as the roots of a tree, filling up all the spaces between sleeping and waking. Memories like groundwater, pulling roots down through her darkness.

NEW HOUSE

SUNRISE. A tree like a broken fountain pumping a jet of frozen branches into the sky, long blue shadows corrugated to map the canaliculate surfaces of the field. Tiny birds catching flame in the branches of the caraganas where Emmett is waiting.

They walk out together across the field toward the new houses. Grass whips stiffly against the cuffs of their pants, snow shin-deep in the furrows. Flakes are still coming down and the air is heavy and hushed. There is only the creaking of their boots in the snow. Stace stops and looks back at the house and sees the tracks behind them have vanished. Where they have stepped a moment ago the snow has sifted and filled the holes left by their boots, erasing every trace of their passage.

Emmett touches Stace's elbow. We don't have much time, he says.

They pass the dumpster and the stolen red truck with its cap of snow, follow a track of boot prints up one of the driveways, the prints little more than faint indentations in the snow.

Wind has made a low drift at the corner of the house, and Emmett pushes the garage door open and steps over the ridge of snow into the garage. He bangs snow off his parka and pushes the door closed behind Stace, stamps his feet. Grey light filters through the half wagon wheel window at the top of the slide-up garage door. Their boots shed cleats of snow on the concrete floor.

It's in the living room, Emmett says.

Stace follows Emmett up into the house and along a dim passageway to the living room. Through the archway he sees one naked foot and then his old hiking boots. One of the boots tipped on its side as if it has been kicked off and forgotten.

He leans against the arch and looks into the living room. The man is lying curled on the floor with his face turned away.

Emmett pushes past him and slings the nylon tote onto the table saw and removes the camera from the bag, loads a new film pack.

Take off your coveralls, Emmett says. You won't be needing those where you're going.

Stace sees the empty syringe and the crumpled square of foil and the orange sheath of the needle. He steps into the room and kneels in the sawdust beside the body. The jacket is draped over the body as if the man had been chilled and simply fallen asleep, one bare arm stretched out from under the jacket. A dirty white sock, wrapped loosely around the bicep, trapped between arm and chest.

In the ashy light, the man's face is discoloured, blood dead beneath skin. Stace puts out a hand and touches a stubbled, icy cheek. It is his own collapsed face he is looking at. It is no trick of the light.

You have to get out of those coveralls, Emmett says again.

Stace unlaces the borrowed hiking boots and kicks them off his feet, unzips the coveralls to his waist and steps naked out of them.

Emmett sits down across the room and leans against the wall and brings the camera up to his eye.

Stace looks to Emmett, afraid now. Something has opened beneath him and he sees there is no bottom to this. He is doubled, split in two, looking down into himself as if from a height.

Lie down, Emmett says.

Stace lies down on the floor and it is the right thing to do and he feels a calmness come over him where a moment before there had been only fear. He slips one arm beneath the familiar denim jacket and pulls in close behind the still body. The collar of the jacket smelling of his tobacco, the oils of his own hair. His hand brushes over the corner of the postcard in the breast pocket of the shirt. He flattens his nose into the secret hollow at the base of the skull.

He has thrown his life away out of carelessness and out of stupidity. Now he knows this and it is too late.

He feels lightheaded and when he closes his eyes he sees he is standing in the kitchen of his father's old apartment and he is looking at his father sitting at the table. His father spreads fragments of bloodied glass over the surface of the table. Each piece aligned precisely as if according to an invisible grid.

SUNDAY MORNING 7

JACK-LIGHTING

HE IS WIRED ABOVE MY HEAD. This photograph is my father. Everything is naked around him.

My father's love was not love. Now I can see my father more clearly, even though he is much further from me. What can I say about him that has not already been said about every father? I will not tell you about his hands, which were so big he could carry in one palm an entire globe of pain the size of a fist. His fists which knocked down doors and went through glass as though cutting only air, his fists still fists on the bloody newspaper spread over the kitchen table where I tweezered glass from between his knuckles and from the backs of his hands.

The summer I left home he worked afternoons and evenings as a stock clerk in the IGA across the street. Railway Avenue. Behind the IGA, where we couldn't see them, the railroad tracks ran in four parallel sets, and beyond that, up a bit of a hill, was the highway. From the kitchen window in our apartment you could see the lights at the intersection change, and hear the big rigs downshift when they were slowing up to the intersection, and then the roar of the diesels as they went through the lights and cranked up for the climb out of the river valley. Our living room windows—there were three of them—looked over 100th Avenue. Our apartment was on the third floor, over the newspaper office and stationery store, right on the corner, so we were always looking down at the T-intersection of Railway and 100th. When you looked straight out the living room windows, you were looking at the Cecil Hotel, which I think is the kind of hotel every city has near the railroad tracks. There was a bar there on the corner, with a door that swung inward to a cool, beer- and smoke-flavoured darkness, which my father for some reason boycotted and, at the back of the hotel, with a newer glass door which opened onto 100th, was the off-sales, next to the alley.

My father grew African violets. Barricaded in front of the living room windows, which got light from the east in the morning, he had brown folding card tables set up permanently. The furry-leaved plants gave him some kind of comfort, I guess, but I know they were also a hassle. He'd come home from a shift and I'd hear him banging the kitchen cabinets as he got down a glass for the whiskey and a plate and cutlery for a late dinner, and then he'd go into the living room and set his plate on a corner of the plant table and sit down and eat in front of the plants. Most evenings he brought home half a roast chicken and some cooked vegetables from the store, and he'd have one glass of whiskey, rarely more. As he ate, he'd pluck dead leaves from the violets and otherwise fuss a bit with the plants. Then he'd turn off the lights and sit in darkness at the window and watch the off-sales. It was a habit he had. He'd sit in the darkened living room, eating the roast chicken, and watch the young men parked in front of the bar. The cars would come by all evening, until the off-sales closed around midnight, and they'd park for maybe five minutes, and one or two of the people from the car would go up the cement steps and into the bar, and whoever was left in the car, usually women or girls, would listen to the radio or music on the stereo, and their voices and the music would come up to our window. My father hated those kids, particularly the punks, as he called the boys. He had volunteered for the war, and he'd gone over and been shot through the leg and sent home again, all by the time he was the same age as the kids down there in front of the bar, and he never gave a reason for it, but his disgust was clear to me. My father was a tall straight man and people at times mistook him for a cowboy, but it was anger that kept him thin, not hard work outdoors.

Some of the kids, the younger ones, about my age, he saw with their mothers in the IGA, helping with the grocery shopping after school. The older ones, singly or in pairs, would come in later in the evening to do their shopping, and sometimes they were a bit drunk or stoned, and that kind of behaviour irritated my father, and on evenings when he had been subjected to some annoyance at the store, he'd come home and drink and not say anything. Those kids don't know shit, he'd say on other occasions. He'd overhear their conversations as they walked down the aisles in the store. I hope you're getting a better education than they are, he'd say to me. He had dropped out after grade eight, to work. I was failing school, and that seemed to give him the justification he needed to cut me off, so that we spent most of the time we were at home together in silence.

The only thing we really did together as father and son was fish. For that we didn't need words. In the summer, he'd come home from work some nights and want to go fishing. The IGA stayed open late, so it would always be dark when he finished his shift. I'd gather together the rods and the plastic ice bag he used to carry the fish in, and the heavy red six-volt lantern we kept at the bottom of the hall closet, and he'd take a can of corn niblets or a bag of miniature coloured marshmallows, and we'd walk through the darkened streets of the town to the river. There was a new bridge over the river, for the big rigs going north through town instead of west, and we'd cross the bridge and hop over the guard rail at the far end and scramble down the embankment a bit and then duck under the bridge.

It was sometime in August, I think, the end of a long week of heat. I remember the smell of the musk oil my father wore that evening against the mosquitoes. The river ran black and loud under the bridge, and together we tied leaders on our lines, a white and red float at the top and small lead weights with brass eyes at the end of the line, and a triple set of small hooks that we baited with the corn or marshmallows. We stood on the concrete abutment with our heads almost touching the underside of the bridge deck, and below us the river swirled slow and deep, between the bank and the first pier. Whenever a car or truck passed overhead we would both instinctively duck, the whole deck vibrating above us.

As soon as the lines were ready, I took the net and the flashlight and skidded down the clay bank to the foot of the concrete support, and eased my way out on the weed-slimed rocks immediately below my father. Keep coming, he called from overhead, until he could see I was in position, and I turned the lantern onto the water and shone it down, the water suddenly revealed as murky green shot through with flecks of brown, and we could see the fish schooling in the deep slack water in an eddy beside the pier. Moths fluttered in the cone of our light, and from beneath the girders of the bridge, bats flicked like torn black paper, swooping low over the river.

He cast first one line then the other into the pool of lighted water and fish would swim up toward the surface, see the bait on the invisible lines, and strike. We caught three or four fish in a half hour with the jack-light, and my father reeled the fish in, angling the line toward me, and I held the aluminum handle of the net out over the water until I could scoop it under the fish and bring them in to shore. I had the steel fish chain anchored in the shallows among the stones, and I'd press their jaws open and slip the steel shank through the mouth and out the pink, flared gills. The fish already strung out on the chain would flip and wriggle as I lowered the whole thing back into the water. The lantern was tied on a lanyard around my neck, so the netting of the fish, the unhooking and chaining was all done in intermittent light, the beam of the flashlight shooting around the space below the bridge as I scrambled to catch hold of the line.

In that way we saw the rubber inner tube coming down the river. At first I heard nothing, as the river was so loud, and I was so close to the water, but my father saw it, and called down to me to put out the light. I switched off the lantern and looked up at him and he was crouched on the edge of the concrete above my head and looking out over the river. I turned to follow his gaze and I saw the inner tube, a big one from a tractor, twirling slowly down the centre of the river, with maybe three or four kids on it. One of them had a flashlight, the beam of light playing over the trees on the far bank of the river. Their voices carried over to us but I couldn't make out what they were saying but they were laughing and when they passed under the bridge, on the far side of the pier, where we couldn't see them, a couple of them let out whoops which echoed under the bridge and then the tube was visible again, being carried swiftly away from us and away from the town on the black back of the river.

Goddamn punks, I heard my father say, and then he collapsed the fishing rods in the dark and I picked up the chain of fish and put them in the plastic bag.

I'm coming down, he said. Shine the light up here. I turned the lantern up the slope, showing him the path where I had made my way down to the river's edge, and he picked his way down, holding both rods in his left hand like a balancing act, and grabbing onto roots and even the clay for support. Then he was standing on the rocks beside me and I could smell the sweat and the musk on him. He had been drinking in the darkness above me and whiskey was thick on his breath.

How'd we do? he asked. I showed him the fish in the bag.

He looked upriver to the low shelving bank where the fire pit was, where the shallows lay. A dirt track wide enough for a car led down from the highway, curving through the underbrush between the huge cottonwoods and one or two picnic tables that had been donated by the Lions Club. It was a kind of unofficial park. In the daytime mothers would walk down from town with their children to play in the mud at the edge of the river, and most summer evenings there would be families there, sitting around a bonfire, because the bush had been cut or burnt back and the ground was open in that place and a breeze from the river usually kept the mosquitoes off, but this night it was too late for families.

The raft had come from somewhere up there, around the bend in the river, and we could see an electric light glinting through the bush. If a car had come down to the picnic area while we were fishing, there was a chance we would not have noticed it at all, given the masking noise of the river and the angle of the embankment.

We started up the river toward the light. Walking along the bottomland beside the rushing water, the air was plagued with mosquitoes. At knee height the scrubby willows and poplars were ringed with matted debris from spring floods, dead leaves and grass in fibrous clumps that could be pulled apart into brown dust and torn leaf meal. The river was low now, and we walked on hard mud and dried out rocks below the clay cut bank which marked the height of the spring channel. Why did we choose to walk up the river? It must have been curiosity. We started up together and nothing was said between us, he carrying the rods and I the bag of dying fish.

A hundred metres or so past the picnic area we found where the kids had launched the tube raft. Three pairs of running shoes had been piled on a flat rock by the water's edge, and someone had left a pair of pants draped over a bush. Empty beer cans had been trodden into the mud around the rock, and the embers of a small fire glowed among the stones. My father cursed and kicked the remains of the fire into the water and looked up the bank. A path had been worn down the face of the clay, and above us we could see the dome light of a car through the bush. A radio was playing quietly.

Let's see what the hell's going on up there, he said then, and I could hear the anger in his voice. Maybe it was about the fire left carelessly on the edge of the river, the litter of beer cans. I cannot say what he was thinking. In the car above us someone waited, listening to the radio. I followed him up the bank and into the clearing with the car.

The girl was lying in the back of the car with her legs out the door. She had no shoes on, just the bottom of one dirty foot touching the ground. Someone had taken her dress and pulled it up over her hips. The dome light was on, moths flicking soft as powder against the plastic cover as the car sat there in the bush with the girl in it and no one around.

We stood for maybe a full long minute without moving, looking at the girl passed out in the car, and then my father uncapped the whiskey and swallowed and then swallowed again before handing the flask to me without a word. He glanced up at the moon and then back down to the river and it seemed like he was working something over in his mind.

He set the rods down and got in the back seat between the girl's legs and I said nothing. I didn't call him back. I stood there and felt something tear open inside me and at that moment, when we had started something that couldn't be undone, I saw my father clearly for the first time. There was the night and the whiskey and the girl and we were distant as two planets, my father and I, and yet I was a part of him and carried within me his lightness and all his darkness. What little remained of my childhood was being burned out of me and the knowledge of that was fierce and bitter and exciting. What I lost that night I cannot say.

I went and sat on the hood with my feet crossed and my back against the windshield. Turn that fucking light off, he said. I got off the car and opened the front passenger door and switched the dome light off. He had his pants down around his knees and he was kneeling above the girl, touching her between the legs. Get out of the car and leave me the hell alone, he said. Come back in a bit. I closed the car door and went over to sit against the trunk of a tree. I could see his ass and the bottoms of his shoes through the open door. The girl's legs were sticking out so he couldn't close the door. It would have been too hot in there with the door closed anyway.

After a while I heard him talking to the girl in a low voice but I never heard her say a thing, and then he crawled quickly out of the car backwards and tucked the tail of his shirt into his pants and did up the buckle of his belt.

Alright, he said. I got up from the ground and went over to the car. I touched the girl's leg. It was smooth and still, the skin so beautiful that I started to cry. Don't start up with that shit, he said. He put a hand on the back of my head and pushed me down so I had to get inside the car. The seat under the girl's ass was wet and slippery. Do it, he said behind me. She don't care what you do. He turned on the light above me.

I put my mouth down to her stomach, her belly like a white cake in the moonlight. He walked away from the car a bit, leaving me with the girl. I touched her lips, which were wet and smelled of alcohol. I laid against her for a while, feeling her breath on my cheek, trying to wake her up, saying things in her ear, but she made no motion or sound. After a few minutes he came back and leaned against the side of the car and said, You done? and I eased back along the seat until I could put my feet down to the ground and he said, You pussy, couldn't even fuck her, you're too soft. I walked around the front of the car and puked, the whiskey hot inside my chest and my throat, and he said, The cops can tell who puked if they get that stuff under a microscope in the lab. I found a paper wrapper from a waffle cone in the grass and knelt and scraped the puke and dirt into the paper with the edge of a cigarette box.

We left the car up there above us, the doors open and the small yellow light shining down on the blue vinyl seats and the girl. Night pooled all around the dusty, glowing windows of the car. The radio was tuned to a country station, an old song I wish I could forget the words to. We slid down the bank and the piping of frogs from the reeds shut off like a switch. The surface of the river was open to the moonlight. Somehow I had lost the lantern, and we splashed out into the shallows where there was light on the water, our jeans soaked to the knees, above us a black lacework of branches against the hard night sky and the stars. Drowned leaves floated past our legs, almost invisible in the choked black water.

Far off, across the river and the fields, we could hear the whine of trucks on the highway, see their lights flickering along a tunnel of trees to vanish around a distant curve long after the sound had faded from hearing.

What are we going to do now? I asked. My fingers were hooked tightly in the back of his belt, holding on to him in the darkness. I clung to him and I hated him.

I needed an answer, but there was none.

Later, I was in the middle of a field. My father was kneeling before me, his hands on his knees. Something was dripping from his mouth.

I will not forget this.

SUPER 8

THE FIRST SHOT swings up and catches her below the waist as she stands in the doorway. The camera focuses in on the faded cotton of a sundress, a straw purse. A hand comes down into the top of the picture, and then the camera starts to pan with her as she moves across the porch and down the steps. She walks into the frame, stops, stares at the camera, and then does something funny with her hair, pushes it up on top of her head, laughs. Shakes her hair out. My father said I have her laugh. I guess that is how they live on in us, in small things like a laugh sometimes. The camera swings away, focusing across the yard to the man sitting on the car. He is wearing his old combat boots and a white T-shirt and his hair is slicked back with pomade like they used to wear it in those days. The woman marches back into the picture, her boots slicing through the silver grass, the purse swinging out from her body with each mock military goose step. The man slides off the car, a big

Pontiac I think it was, though the picture is unclear, and his heels hit the ground together and he ceremoniously bows and opens a door. The woman tilts above the car door, kisses the man on the mouth. She turns to blow a kiss toward the camera, and then the man pushes her down and into the car. He motions silently at the camera. Waving it back. The camera closes in until the man's face fills the frame. The picture freezes, trapping him with his mouth open and a strand of hair coming down over his forehead. When I close my eyes, it is this image I see.

The camera jerks sideways, releasing my father's face. Pulls back slowly across the yard.

At the corner of the porch, a boy is tossing a ball against the side of the house. He watches the car pull away from the yard. Grey dust hangs high in the shifting air. The boy turns, scowling at the camera, cocks his arm as if to throw the ball directly at the lens.

That's me with the ball.

This is my earliest memory.

PRAIRIE SKY

I SAY, I LOVE WATCHING YOU COME and she says, Last time I banged my head on the TV and I say, Let me feel. We were getting supper ready, and the screen door was open. It must have been about four or five o'clock and there was a cool push of air into the kitchen and with it the smell of rain.

That's one thing I love about the prairies: a late afternoon sky darkening like silver and slats of sun low and green on the fields and hills, and everything very visible from every direction — every fence post and piece of gravel on the highway, every tree still and living inside itself. And then the leaves turning up silver undersides when that first cool wind comes down from the hills carrying the smell of rain and damp earth, lifting up the leaves and the clothes on the line and banging a shutter against the side of the house.

She says, I should get the wash in, because there are sheets to fold, and I say, We'd both better. She pulls a shirt on and jams her feet into a pair of old runners. How do I look? she asks.

I kiss her neck as she buttons the shirt. She laughs and twists away, pushes the screen door open with her hip, tucking in the shirt with both hands. Come on, the rain will be here any moment, she says. Standing on the porch looking at me. Come on. Behind her the yard, the clothesline vibrating, the clothes leaping up white as surprise.

Maybe one day I will be able to come back to this afternoon and see it for the first time and know none of what comes after. Like you, reading it now on this page.

SUNDAY MORNING 8 LATE

CAUL

THE CAUL HAS SEALED OVER the face and Emmett gets up from the floor and he sees that the process is almost complete. Soon the entire head will be covered by the waxy, translucent membrane.

Of all of it, this is the part he likes best. The transfer. The hands twitching blindly as if to open a space in something unseen in the room. Emmett stands over the two bodies with the camera and already the naked body is dissolving into the other. Emmett pulls the safety tab and presses the shutter release. First the limbs and then the torso, sinking from sight like water through sand. He pulls the tab and puts the polaroid on the table saw, takes another picture, the flash bouncing off the bare walls. Then the rest of the body goes, everything at once, and last the head in its white shroud. He snaps a final picture. He is left in the room with the jean-clad corpse of a man under a jacket. A thermostat has shut off the furnace, and the house is silent but for the voices of dead friends in the wind under the eaves.

He peels the polaroids apart and looks at the images before slipping the photographs into the notebook. He looks around the room one last time. Mullioned windows throw rhomboids of shadow across the wall and the floor and body on the floor. It is a room like any other. The white coveralls he rolls into a bundle and jams in the bag. He picks up the spare hiking boots and walks out of the house and back across the winter field to the van.

POLICE

LILLIS RAE AWAKES and the room comes in slowly; the white of the bedspread dimly ridged, her clothes on the floor where she must have dropped them in the night. Her head pounds and her mouth is parched. A hangover, she thinks. She looks at the bedside clock and remembers the whiskey. She rolls over and swings her feet out, pulls underwear on and then jeans and shirt. Her work socks still on her feet. She gets out of the bed and opens the curtains and slips a wool sweater on in front of the window. The yard is still and frozen beneath a small haloed sun, a cap of new snow on the roof of the International Travelall since yesterday afternoon.

She uses the bathroom quickly, without turning on the light, goes down to the living room.

The surface of the coffee table is littered with photographs torn from albums. She splits the drapes with one tug and winter light floods in. At first even that is too bright and she closes her eyes against it and when she opens them she sees the ring on her finger. She turns the ring around her knuckle and puts her hand flat to the wavy glass.

Grosbeaks have found the mountain ash in front of the house. The birds shake the branches with the violence of their attack. Black on yellow and white, the air quick with wings, the morning shrinking to the size of a remembered voice. Something like honey on the back of her hand.

The photographs have been destroyed. His face scratched out of every picture, emulsion scraped back to the paper beneath. The remaining photographs glued together by spilled rye.

She leaves the photographs and picks up the beer bottles and the whiskey and carries the empties into the kitchen.

She finds the ashtray with Tanya's cigarettes by the sink. She sets the bottles on the kitchen counter and lights the stove, rinses the ashtray under the tap before filling the kettle. From a cupboard she takes down a thermos. Pins her nametag to her shirt. Putting the day together. Behind her, on the stove, the enamel kettle creaks on the heat. The water comes to a boil and she makes a full pot, looking out over the yard as she drinks a coffee at the table. The ring a cold band of silver under her hand.

She has forgotten so many things that when she does remember them, it's not in her head but in her whole body—the touch, the movement, the soft spirit of light. Soon he will be nothing but memory, she thinks, and he will slip away from me. She had always thought the past receded forever, losing details first and then even the crudest outlines in the far distance. Now she sees memories revolving her like satellites, each memory in its own orbit, spinning away, only to—at the moment of furthest apogee—come back again closer and closer, tattered and misshapen by its travels through time. Details, unnoticed before, becoming significant: a word, a gesture, a hand softly touching a shoulder, things seen and now understood; and then the past arcing silently away on its secret trajectories.

She pours the pot of coffee into the thermos and opens the back door, ice cracking down the frame, switches the porch light off. Cold air floods across the kitchen floor. Snow has drifted in the night beneath the screen, the frozen rubber doorskirt scraping snow in an arc as she steps into the closed-in porch. She locks the kitchen door behind her, sets the thermos on the hutch to pull a down vest over her sweater, the red vest patched with duct tape where she caught it on barbed wire.

She stands on the steps, tilting her head to look up at the brottled ceiling of cloud. In the thermometer, she can see the mercury has dropped overnight, her breath clouding white, the size of a lung. The screen door slaps behind her. She goes down the steps to the yard and listens at the bottom of the stairs. The yard is silent, wood smoke standing up above the line of the roof. Snow crisp beneath her boots as she steps onto the lawn.

A sober-headed chickadee quiet in the branches above her.

She lifts the orange electrical extension cord from the bumper of the International Travelall and shakes the snow free before unplugging the block heater and draping the stiff extension cord over the porch railing. With her elbow she scrapes snow from the truck door, the truck blanketed in white.

She starts the truck, letting it warm while she bangs snow off the hood and the roof of the cab with a broom. Heavy snow slides clear of the windshield when she gets back in and turns on the wipers. There is nothing but static on the radio.

She backs the truck around in the yard and drives past the side of the house and down the long drive and out to the road. The camber of the road is leveled by unbroken snow, a flat cover with no drifting. The grass in the ditches is silver and broken in the weak sunlight. From a snowy bush along the fence she flushes a ruffed grouse low across the road.

The red truck she sees first, and then she sees the white and blue police 4x4 parked up at the new show homes. On the driveway by the dumpster, two workers standing beside their van, both smoking and both talking on cell phones. A policeman is stretching yellow crime tape across the front of one of the houses. The red truck has already been cordoned off, yellow tape wrapped around pylons on the snow. She slows down and looks out the side window as she goes past, but from this distance, she can't tell what is happening at the house. She heard nothing last night, she is certain of that.

SNOW

He has tramped out a clearing on the higher ground, among the mullein stalks and clumps of potentilla, and spread a plastic bag to sit. Shale digs into his knees. He unzips the nylon bag and brings out a creased box of crackers, a tin of herring. With the blade of a knife he spears herring into his mouth, the oily brown fish tasting of tin. He eats slowly, shaking crackers one by one from the box as he watches the yard.

A woman in a red vest comes down from the house and it is impossible to see her face, though he can tell it is her. She cleans snow off the truck and climbs up into the cab and closes the door. The sound carries up to him a moment later.

The truck goes down the drive past the house, flashing through the caragana hedge, turns onto the road. At the new subdivision the truck slows and almost stops but does not.

He watches the truck until it is gone from sight, the road itself lifting silvered a moment then sinking back, swallowed by the curve of land. It is snowing again. The pale trees at the far edge of her field like a shaken curtain of grey. A long drifting veil slants down across the road and the fields, and the grasses pitch in the wind, the earth turning slowly to white below him.

He finishes eating. Sparrows flush like dun shadows through the barbed wire of the boundary fence and into the steeplebush where he has thrown the empty herring tin. Tiny insects, sheltered beneath rosettes of soft mullein leaves, rise briefly into chill air when he stands to go.

I gratefully acknowledge the financial assistance of the Explorations Program of the Canada Council, and the Ontario Arts Council Writers' Reserve Program.

Portions of this manuscript appeared in somewhat different form in the anthologies, *Red Stains* and *Dust*, both from Creation Books of England.

Thanks to my editor, Brian Kaufman, for having faith, and also to Michael Kenyon and Stuart Ross, for advice and encouragement. And special thanks to Bonnie Light for tireless support, and her eagle eyes. With her help, this book was finally possible.

The Beautiful Dead End original soundtrack recording available on CD.

www.clinthutzulak.com